Grey

SHEEP'S (

Austin Lee was a maverick clergyman, a thorn in the side of the Church of England, of which he outspokenly despaired. He was a staunch socialist, pacifist and a colourful and stirring preacher, and wrote widely and controversially in the press on politics and social issues.

Born in Keighley in 1904 and educated at Cambridge, Wells and Oxford, he moved frequently from parish to parish, mainly in Lincolnshire and London, and was also briefly a naval chaplain in the 1930s.

In 1955 he turned his talents to fiction, creating Miss Flora Hogg, a former school mistress turned Private Investigator, and wrote other detective novels under the pseudonyms John Austwick and Julian Callender.

He never married, and died in 1965.

SHEEP'S CLOTHING

A Detective Frolic

AUSTIN LEE

Greyladies

Published by
Greyladies
an imprint of The Old Children's Bookshelf

© The Estate of Austin Lee 1955

This edition first published 2015
Design and layout © Shirley Neilson 2015

ISBN   978-1-907503-49-8

Set in Sylfaen / Perpetua
Printed and bound by the CPI Group (UK) Ltd,
Croydon CR0 4YY

SHEEP'S CLOTHING

For
HILDA M. LEE
and
MARGARET WELLS

CHAPTER 1

W<small>HEN</small> Superintendent Hogg died in the late '40s, there was nothing to prevent his daughter, Flora, from realizing an ambition which had been simmering in her mind for quite a number of years. Her Christian name she owed to the romantic temperament of her mother, who had predeceased the Superintendent by ten years, a temperament which Flora had in no small measure inherited, though it had remained undiscovered by the majority of the pupils at the Surrey County School where she had been teaching French since before the war. In appearance she was moderately tall, had once had flaming red hair, a reminder of her Stirlingshire ancestry, now toning to a dull copper, and on her somewhat aggressive nose she balanced a pair of pince-nez.

The Superintendent died early in January, with a consideration he had always shown to his subordinates, so that there was still one day after his cremation at Mortlake, a ceremony attended by an impressive gathering of the County Constabulary, including the Chief Constable himself, for Miss Hogg to compose and make a fair copy of the term's notice she was required to give on desiring to relinquish her post. The headmistress had received her resignation with regret, tempered by the knowledge that at least fifty applicants were ready, furnished with nine copies each of three indubitably laudatory testimonials from the Principal of their Training College, their previous headmistress, and of the Vicar at home, to step into the vacant appointment.

Miss Hogg got through the term with no outward sign to reveal the momentous decision she had arrived at. She said good-bye to her colleagues, her pupils and the headmistress, received with suitable expressions of gratification

1

a quite expensively fitted dressing-case with which they marked their appreciation of her past efforts for the school, and departed to fulfil a minor ambition, for she had never before felt able to resign her father into the somewhat chapped hands of the daily woman, by going on a conducted tour of Italy. It was not a great success. Spring had delayed its journey to the Apennines, there was fog in Milan, a flurry of snow obscured the decaying glory of Rome, and although the cold kept in check the smells of Venice, the necessity for the constant use of an umbrella interfered with the larger perspectives. Worst of all, Miss Hogg was a confirmed potterer who loved idling in market-places, in piazzas, before shops that sold every variety of *bondieuseries*. But the guide, a Mr. Dalrymple on vacation from Cambridge, had an almost religious determination to prevent Satan's being provided with idle hands, or it may simply have been a Marxist aversion from individual aberrations from the norm. Whatever it was, Miss Hogg found herself treated as a member of a herd, dragooned from the Vatican to the Pincian Gardens, and from the Academia to the Pineta and San Apollinare in Classe. To the end of her life she was never able to remember whether it was Vergil or Dante whose tomb she had gazed upon through an iron grille in a street of Ravenna, and Matthew Arnold's poem which would have settled the matter for her was not among the lyrical and elegiac verses selected by Palgrave for his pioneer anthology, which had been a set book in Miss Hogg's training year.

She arrived back in South Green on the last Friday in April, spent the week-end making the front room of her little house in Acacia Avenue look as much like an office as possible, a task which the late Superintendent's wallpaper negatived from the start, and on the Monday, just before eight o'clock in the morning she screwed, a trifle defiantly, a small brass plate into the middle of the front door. It had been engraved for her before she went away and read simply:

MISS HOGG, B.A.
Private Investigator

The words, although admirably concise, had only been arrived at after a process of long and careful cogitation. 'Detective' or ' Private Detective' she had rejected as being a little too assertive considering her amateur status even if she had been born not in the purple but at least in the blue; 'Private Eye', a term she was familiar with from her extensive acquaintance with American thrillers, was too flamboyant, and probably unintelligible to the majority of those whom she hoped to rope in as her clientele; and 'Confidential Enquiries' seemed too redolent of the Divorce Court which she hoped, except in the extreme of financial embarrassment, to avoid. She had already posted a letter to the Telephone Manager asking for a black entry in the next issue of the Telephone Directory, which she trusted would appear some time within the next two years, and she had sent copies of an advertisement to several newspapers, the wording of which she had scribbled down in the Café Florian at Venice while she listened with half an ear to Mr. Dalrymple's story of the fall of the Campanile just out of sight at the end of the piazza.

Miss Hogg, B.A. Private Investigator.
Confidential Enquiries of every description undertaken. Ring South Green 1212.

She was, she well knew, extremely fortunate in her telephone number, and her academic status (she had

3

taken Modern Languages at Bristol) was a guarantee of a certain personal ability, if not necessarily in the fields of forensic science.

It was a mild spring morning, much milder than it had been in those awful pine woods where Vergil – or was it Dante? – had once gathered violets. Miss Hogg surveyed her front door with approval. She picked up the hammer, which she had not needed in the event, the screwdriver and the metal knitting-needle which she had used to make the preliminary openings for the screws, and went inside to make some toast. With the latest exploit of Henry Gamadge propped against the milk-jug she made a hearty breakfast of toast and dripping. Then, having washed up, for the daily woman had, on the Superintendent's decease, become biweekly, she went into the front room and sat at her desk, a large roll-top affair which the Superintendent had once used for keeping his records of pigeon-racing, a sport to which he had been much addicted in his youth.

For a time she toyed with the various directories and reference books which she had installed the previous Saturday, filled her fountain-pen, and moved the client's chair a little nearer to the desk. Then she sat and sucked the end of her pen. The County Girls' School would be just filing in to prayers. How satisfactory it was not to be sitting on the platform, listening to Miss Gribbling announcing the hockey results of the previous Saturday: 'Now, although they didn't quite manage to win, yet I think we ought to give them a clap for the really sporting effort.' And yet, a tiny qualm seized her. What would happen if she never had a client?

'Don't be so silly, Hogg,' she admonished herself. She never used her Christian name if she could avoid it, nor did her best friends. 'No one knows about you yet. You'll be smothered in work before you know where you are. Even if it's only divorce work,' she added candidly. And

4

thereupon she took up the pen she had just filled and wrote a long letter to her bosom friend, Millicent Brown, a spinster of independent means who lived in an Essex cottage, and wrote stories for children which appeared each year in the older-fashioned Christmas annuals. Moral support was what she needed at the moment, and it would be nice to have Milly to stay for a week or two.

CHAPTER 2

SOUTH GREEN was still a village at the beginning of the 1914 war. In living memory, people in the cottages along the Barbrook had plaited baskets from the osiers and sold them in Brentford market. But progress was on the way, and by 1920 the Barbrook had gone underground and become part of the South London sewerage system, for South Green, although geographically in Surrey, had become a suburb of the metropolis. The centre of South Green, bordering on the eponymous area of grass which now kept a Council employee in full-time employment divesting it of newspapers, cigarette packets, sweet papers and ice-cream cartons, and even nastier debris of modern urban civilization, was still a well-to-do residential quarter. Here lived an unfashionable baron, son of a Victorian Lord Chief Justice, the widow of an Edwardian ambassador, several knights, an American expatriate – a mysterious gentleman of presumably independent means who had bought Barbrook Lodge soon after the end of the war, but returned no calls and was at home to no one, and Mr. Bartley Craig, the writer of whimsical articles in women's periodicals and nostalgic novels of Public School life. The modern world, however, was encroaching. In spite of agonized protests, of letters to *The Times* and the *Surrey, South Green and Twickenham Observer*, a block of flats had gone up fronting the Green on the South Side, not a hundred yards from the residence of Lord Hounslow, and a further block, already on the drawing-boards, was projected for the West Side when old Lady Martyngale, the ambassador's widow, should have ceased to require an earthly *pied-à-terre* or, at least, anything like so large a one as she was at present occupying.

6

The church, dedicated for some unknown reason to St. Bombast, an obscure Cornish saint of doubtful historicity, was an Italianate structure replacing an earlier building at the north corner of the Green which had stood derelict from the middle of the eighteenth century. In those days South Green had been in the archdiocese of Canterbury and, as is well known, Archbishops are too busy with the weightier affairs of State to be able to devote very much of their time to pastoralia. South Green had fallen an easy prey to the Methodists until the Chief Baron, a typical Victorian who, among his many other activities found time to be President of the Anglican Home Missionary Society, had rebuilt the church in the 1870s. Lord Hounslow had had a horror of the High Church movement which, towards the latter half of the nineteenth century was definitely becoming unsound politically, and as Pugin had been fashionable with the Tractarians, the Gothic was anathema to his lordship. So it was that St. Bombast, South Green, was a tolerable copy in little of the basilica of St. John Lateran. The architect had made a good job of it, even down to the holy water stoups let into the walls at the entrances. Happily Lord Hounslow had had no very meticulous acquaintance with the practice of Romanism, and if he had noticed them he had doubtless imagined that they were something to do with the ventilation.

The Vicarage was just on the edge of the fashionable area, half-way down Barbrook Drive. It had been built in 1875 by the anonymous architect at that time in the employment of the Ecclesiastical Commissioners, though a theory is current in ecclesiastical circles that the Commissioners at that time did not waste money on architects' fees, but designed the buildings themselves in their spare time. A fantasy in red and purple brick, in a definitely Gothic mode, it suffered from two main defects: its windows were more mullions than glass so that even in the height of summer the interior was for ever wrapped in a sepulchral twilight; and the foundations had been so sketchily contrived that the rear wall of the house had already sunk more than a foot into the ground. The Vicar, the Reverend Mr. Earwicker, was at the moment paying £78 a year in dilapidations to the Diocesan Board, and if the wall were to be underpinned, this sum would most probably have to be considerably increased.

On the Monday morning, perhaps a quarter of an hour after the time that Miss Hogg had affixed the brass plate to her door, the Vicar was coming down to breakfast. The best adjective to describe him would be colourless, for the parochial clergyman today, if he wishes to remain in favour with his superiors in the ecclesiastical hierarchy, must aspire to a drab mediocrity.

The Church of England has certainly interpreted Catholicity in a wider sense than Rome, and is so comprehensive that it includes ritualists who regard the Holy Father as definitely Low Church, and bishops who do not subscribe to a single dogma of the Oecumenical Councils. Mr. Earwicker belonged to what is known as the Moderate school, though if he had been asked to describe himself, he would probably have used the term Prayer Book Catholic. This school makes the best of both worlds, for it enjoys the embellishments which the High Church party have imported into the Anglican rite while still retaining the leisure of the more formal Evangelicals. Mr. Earwicker only had to turn out for one service during the week, and that was at 10 a.m. on Wednesdays. But he enjoyed a delightful array of ecclesiastical millinery ranging from a series of chasubles in coloured brocades to a purple cope presented to the parish by the members of the Mothers' Union, in which he yielded nothing in splendour to the Medicis or the Borgias.

His wife, a buxom woman of the no-nonsense school, and his daughter, a dyspeptic child in a gym slip with wire round her top teeth, were already at table waiting for him to say grace which he did after bidding them a hearty good morning. He had seen them both before, indeed he and his wife shared the front bedroom over the drawing-room, but the greeting was an established routine, like grace, which never varied, and to which his family never made any reply. Neither of them, indeed, closed their eyes for grace, Mrs. Earwicker being at the moment engaged in a calculation as to whether there was enough sugar in the bowl for porridge as well as tea, and Joan frankly speculating as to the nature of her father's correspondence.

As soon as grace was over, the Vicar sat down at the head of the table, and picked up the letters which lay at the side of his porridge plate. He picked them up one at a time with his left hand as he stirred his porridge with his right. They were the usual run of circulars, bills and appeals from charitable societies, with one exception, and it was this one which caused him to put down his porridge spoon so that he could split open the expensive-looking envelope with his right thumb. It was addressed from London's newest and flashiest hotel, the Grandiose in Park Lane, and the crest on the left-top corner of the note-paper, repeated from the flap of the envelope, was ducal in its magnificence.

'My dear,' said the Vicar, 'here's the oddest thing. A letter from the Bishop of Tuscon – no, Tucson – asking if we could put him up for a night or two.' Mr. Earwicker looked like a dog that has come into an unexpected bone.

'I thought the Missionary Week was in November,' said Mrs. Earwicker.

'A bishop!' exclaimed Joan, in tones of the very faintest disparagement. The crest on the envelope had aroused in her more exciting anticipations.

'He isn't a missionary bishop,' explained the Vicar, who had now read the letter through twice. Missionary bishops are very small beer in the Church of England, where precedence is accorded first to the income and secondly to the age of the see. 'He's an American.'

'I thought Americans were Christian Scientists,' said Mrs. Earwicker vaguely. 'That's all the sugar we have in the house, Joan, so if you put it all on your porridge there'll be none for your tea.'

'He says he is trying to arrange exchange visits between English and American clergymen, and he saw my name in the *Church Leader*.'

Mr. Earwicker was an assiduous writer to the Church Press, his subjects ranging from the position of aumbries and the necessity of taking the ablutions in the right place to the removal of bats from belfries and the exclusion of cockroaches from parish halls.

'When does he want to come?' asked Mrs. Earwicker.

'Tonight if it can be managed. He says he goes back to the States next week.'

'I'll put a bottle in the spare-room bed after breakfast,' said Mrs. Earwicker. She was accustomed to the descents of strange preachers, assiduously doing the rounds of the English parishes to wheedle alms for the multiplicity of societies which do at least give jobs to clergymen who have no vocation for the pastoral office. 'It'll have to be macaroni cheese and a trifle.'

The Vicar took this reference to the evening collation which his wife proposed to offer the bishop as an oblique indication of the state of the housekeeping money.

'I can let you have ten shillings,' he said. 'One of your rabbit pies would be very nice. The bishop may not be addicted to cheese.'

'He must know about rationing,' said Mrs. Earwicker,

but it was tacitly agreed that rabbit pie should replace macaroni cheese on the menu.

'We might have macaroni cheese afterwards as a savoury,' suggested the Vicar.

'Extravagance I will not countenance,' replied Mrs. Earwicker. 'What with a war, and then a Labour Government, two courses are enough for anybody.'

'Well, do your best, my dear,' said the Vicar absently. He was already building castles or, more strictly speaking, palaces in the air. Did bishops, he wondered, live in palaces in America? It might not be thought to be in accordance with the principles of the purest democracy. The Founding Fathers, he had always understood, were Quakers, or was it Independents? Independents were surely Congregationalists? He must look it up before the bishop arrived. It would not do to be ignorant of the ecclesiastical organization of a country in which he hoped to shine as an itinerant evangelist. There was that series of sermons on *The Commandments of Today*, and the Advent course he had given on the Seven Deadly Sins. Strong meat, but it was the sort of thing that went down, as long as one made it quite clear that the sinner was the other person, not the individual being addressed. That was the secret of successful preaching. He came back to reality to find that Mrs. Earwicker was addressing him.

'I beg your pardon.'

'I said there's the washing to do, whether the bishop's coming or not, so if you want any more tea you must pour it out for yourself.'

'Thank you, my dear,' said the Vicar, a slightly pained note in his voice, implying that his kingdom was not of this world. Mrs. Earwicker's feet were, as he sometimes reflected, a little too mundanely planted on terra firma. But, as she was wont to observe, someone has got to do the work.

'Come along, now, Joan,' she admonished. 'You're going to be late for school.' And then, as a concession to her husband of whom, strangely enough, she was very fond, she said: 'I can make some soup to begin with out of the rabbit bones.'

CHAPTER 3

THE MOST legendary of the residents around the Green was undoubtedly Miss Emily Dewdney, daughter of Sir Arthur Dewdney, the Victorian epigraphist. Although her elder sister had been dead for quite fifteen years she was still referred to in the neighbourhood as Miss Emily, and it seemed only natural, for she carried with her from an earlier age those nice distinctions which vanished for ever between the two wars. Sir Arthur, who had been knighted in the year of the Great Exhibition, had married late in life, almost, as was said at the time, in a fit of absent-mindedness, but this had in no way interfered with his predilection for wandering in the Middle East and even farther afield. His early years had been spent in a search for the Etruscan equivalent of the Rosetta Stone, but, Italy proving too parochial a field, and the Roman marshes too conducive to various distempers, he had gradually exchanged epigraphy for palaeontology, and ended by devoting himself to manuscripts, in search of which he had ransacked the monasteries of the Levant. In 1870, when Miss Emily was three years old, he had died of fever contracted in a remote corner of Azerbaijan. Looking at Miss Emily it was astonishing to think that her father had died eighty years before. In appearance she was tall and thin, her grey hair parted down the middle, and swept into a tight bun at the back. Her eyes were brown, and her glance, as an irreverent tradesman had once remarked to whom she had been complaining about the quality of his poultry, could stop a clock at twenty yards. Invariably she dressed in purple, and whatever the material it was usually trimmed liberally with beads.

On this Monday morning, at half past nine, she emerged from the drive gate of the Laurels – the Council had recently allotted it a number, but Miss Emily refused to take cognizance of the fact – and proceeded towards what she still referred to as the village to do her shopping. Her way led down Barbrook Drive, past the Vicarage, where the Vicar was at that very moment engaged in telephoning the bishop at his Park Lane hotel to say that they would be delighted to welcome him, and then at right angles down Acacia Avenue. There was little that escaped the sharp brown eyes of Miss Emily, and she noted instantly the brass plate that had been newly fixed on the front door of number 33. Wondering if the house could possibly have been taken by a veterinary surgeon, for her cat, Sarah, named after the French actress and so pronounced, was extremely philo-progenitive, and required that kittens should be put to sleep at least three times a year, Miss Emily walked up the path and read the lettering on the plate:

MISS HOGG, B.A.
Private Investigator

'Goodness gracious me!' exclaimed Miss Emily, and immediately put her finger to the bell.

Miss Hogg had just sealed down the envelope enclosing the letter to her friend, Milly Brown, and was inscribing on it the words 'Tolleshunt Darcy', when the bell rang. From the desk she was unable to see the path from the gate to the front door. 'Milk?' she considered. 'I pay on Saturdays. The Vicar? Too early. In any case he never calls on anybody.' That it should be a client did not even cross her mind. She got up and went to the front door.

'Good morning,' she said. She knew Miss Emily by sight, but they had never before met.

'Am I addressing Miss Hogg?' asked Miss Emily.

'That's me. I should say I, of course, but it sounds so pedantic. Won't you come in?'

'It's a little matter of business,' said Miss Emily, on which Miss Hogg, who had momentarily hesitated between the office and the more comfortable sitting-room at the back, led her into the office.

'Very nice,' said Miss Emily approvingly. Her father had had just such a desk, and it was still in the library at the Laurels, and the wallpaper was almost exactly duplicated in the maid's bedroom at the top of the house. 'I saw your plate and I need to consult someone. Something very odd is happening at my house.'

'Odd?' queried Miss Hogg, who had settled herself at the desk, her chair half turned so that she faced Miss Emily in the client's chair on her right. 'In what way?'

'Things have been moved,' replied Miss Emily. 'In the night,' she added, as if this explained everything.

Miss Hogg was a trifle nonplussed.

'What sort of things?' she asked.

'Books,' said Miss Emily vaguely. 'And pictures. And even ornaments.'

'But haven't you a maid who lives with you?'

'Oh, it's not Phyllis Maud,' exclaimed Miss Emily. 'I do all the dusting myself in any case. But I've asked her about the note-book, and the figures in the cabinet, and I'm quite sure she hasn't touched them. In fact I think she's come to the conclusion that I've at last reached my second childhood. She looked at me very strangely this morning.'

'Just tell me exactly what has been happening, and how long it's been going on.'

'Well, to go back to the beginning, that rather effeminate young man, Mr. Bartley Craig, has been coming in on certain afternoons to go through some of Sir Arthur's papers.' Miss Emily always referred to her father in this way, possibly because she had no recollection whatever of him in his paternal capacity. 'He's writing some sort of biography of

15

him to go in a series of Victorian scholars. He wrote to me about a month ago and said he had been commissioned to write Sir Arthur's life, and could he go through some of the books and papers in the library. Of course I said he could, although he didn't seem to me to be at all a suitable choice as a biographer – he writes in those papers for servant girls, you know. Phyllis Maud takes one of them every week. I should have thought a scholar would have been a more appropriate choice, but apparently reading matter has to be very light these days to compete with the wireless and the television. He comes in two or three afternoons a week, and I must say he's been no bother. I told him Phyllis Maud would bring him in a tray of tea, but he wouldn't hear of it. Then last Friday he asked to see me, and when I went into the library he wanted to know if I'd removed some note-book which apparently he'd left on an Indian occasional table at the side of the fireplace the previous afternoon. I told him I hadn't entered the library for some days – I dust it on Tuesdays and Saturdays – and when I rang for Phyllis Maud she was quite emphatic that she had never been near the room, and I believe her. Sir Arthur collected some very odd curios, and among other things there is an Egyptian mummy he once bought at a sale, in a library in a case which looks rather like an open coffin, and Phyllis Maud is terrified of it, so she never does go into the library if she can avoid it.'

'I suppose there was some explanation,' said Miss Hogg, as the other paused. 'Absent-mindedness on Mr. Bartley Craig's part, perhaps.'

'I don't think so,' replied Miss Emily. 'The note-book has never turned up. And then on Saturday Mr. Bartley Craig asked to see me again, and he was considerably agitated. There is a cabinet against one of the walls which holds various pieces of stone and pottery, and a number of Etruscan figurines. Each item is numbered, and there is a catalogue in Sir Arthur's handwriting hanging by a loop of string from the knob of the cabinet door. This catalogue had been taken off the knob and left on a chair, and the exhibits in the cabinet had been considerably disarranged. Again I asked Phyllis Maud about it, and she was quite indignant. I am certain in my own mind that Phyllis Maud knows nothing whatever about it.'

'You have a cat?' asked Miss Hogg.

'Sarah wouldn't have dreamed of such a thing.' Miss Emily raised a gloved hand. 'Besides she is very fully occupied at the moment with her latest family. The father is that dreadful old Tom that belongs to the housekeeper of the flats. And there were other disturbances in the room. A picture had been lifted from the wall near the fireplace and propped against the skirting board. Sarah couldn't possibly have had anything to do with that.'

'Might it be a poltergeist?' asked Miss Hogg wildly.

'Certainly not,' replied Miss Emily, in a tone that said quite plainly she would not allow that sort of thing in her house. 'No, I am afraid the only conclusion I can come to is that someone has been getting into the library from outside.'

'But why? Is there anything particularly valuable in the library?'

'Nothing of any great intrinsic value.' Miss Emily paused, obviously passing in review through her mind the contents of the library. 'Some of Sir Arthur's manuscripts are of a certain importance to scholars, but they could be of no possible interest to a burglar.'

Miss Hogg tapped the end of her pen against her teeth, an irritating habit which she had developed in the lecture-rooms of Bristol. 'So far nothing has actually gone except the note-book?'

'It's difficult to say,' Miss Emily answered. 'You see, Sir Arthur had a large number of trunks and boxes – indeed, quite half a dozen boxes arrived from Armenia nearly two years after he had died. I remember my mother telling me about them, and I don't think anyone ever went properly through them because there was some question of their being the property of the heirs of the man who financed Sir Arthur's last expedition. I certainly never have. There may be objects of value in them, but I consider it very unlikely. Sir Arthur, in the later years, collected nothing but old manuscripts, and most of them look like nothing so much as pieces of dried animal skin, and very dirty.'

'You never can tell,' said Miss Hogg thoughtfully. 'The *Codex Sinaiticus* was found in some old Greek monastery, and the British Government paid the Russians a million pounds for it before the war.'

'That's as may be,' said Miss Emily, waving aside the *Codex Sinaiticus*. 'I don't think Sir Arthur was very interested in the Christian religion. He was what was called a Free Thinker. Such a mistake, I always think, singularity. However, perhaps we had better go through those old boxes, they are still in the library. Actually I suppose it would need some sort of expert. You don't know anything about early manuscripts, do you?'

'Not yet,' replied Miss Hogg, undaunted.

It was obvious that Miss Emily had not yet revealed everything. She settled back in her chair and clasped her gloved hands.

'Now this has happened, I must tell you of one or two other odd things that have occurred lately.' She paused, as if in doubt how to proceed. 'You know Sir Wellington Orde?' she asked.

'My father knew him, of course. I can't say I've ever spoken to him myself.'

'He was the Director of the Royal Metropolitan Museum, you know, and retired here at the beginning of the last war. I called, naturally and Lady Orde returned the call, but we have very little in common, and as the war soon made it impossible to entertain any but one's intimate friends, we saw very little of each other. However, who should call on me one afternoon about a fortnight ago but Sir Wellington Orde himself. And he told me an obvious cock-and-bull story about how he wanted some occupation for his leisure hours, and he had decided to write a life of Sir Arthur.'

'What an odd thing,' exclaimed Miss Hogg, whose glance had strayed to Brewer in the reference shelf. She found herself wondering whether he threw any light on the original cock-and-bull story.

'Very odd indeed,' agreed Miss Emily. 'Not that Sir Arthur hadn't a certain importance in his time, but even in his own field his work must have been largely superseded in the last century – he has been dead, you know, just eighty years.'

'Goodness!' exclaimed Miss Hogg.

'It seems no time at all,' said Miss Emily placidly, 'as you will know when you get to my age.'

'And what did you say to Sir Wellington?'

'I informed him that the work was already being done by Mr. Bartley Craig, and he seemed very much put out. Indeed he got quite agitated, and left most unceremoniously. And then a really astonishing thing happened. An American has recently occupied one of those horrible flats on the Green near poor Lord Hounslow's' – the adjective referred only to his lordship's proximity to the flats – 'and he called to see me just a week ago today. When Phyllis Maud brought his card up I was quite astonished, as I had never even thought of calling on him. Quite apart from his living in the flats, I understand he is a bachelor and an American.'

19

She opened her reticule and took out a small black purse from which she extracted a slip of pasteboard which she handed to Miss Hogg. She read:

PROFESSOR AMOS T. HOADE
Dept. of Comparative Palaeography
University of Minnesota

'I must say he didn't look very much like an American,' said Miss Emily, whose idea of Americans was based on the works of Charles Dickens and the cartoons in *Punch*. 'Almost a gentleman, in fact, though he was wearing a pair of those parti-coloured shoes that office boys wear at week-ends. After a few preliminary courtesies he told me he was over here on a year's leave from his university, and would I have any objection to his examining Sir Arthur's papers?'

'There simply must be something hidden among them,' said Miss Hogg. 'But what can it be, and how have all these people got to know about it?' She took off her pince-nez, rubbed them with her handkerchief, and clipped them into position again, a sign that she was thinking hard. 'I suppose Mr. Bartley Craig is after the same thing, whatever it is.'

'One presumes so,' agreed Miss Emily, 'in the light of subsequent developments.'

'It seems to me,' said Miss Hogg briskly, 'that there are two things to be done immediately. One is to find out what it is they are after, and the other is to guard the library until we are able to forestall them.'

'Excellent,' said Miss Emily. 'I think,' she added practically, 'that you had better come and stay at the Laurels for a few days.'

'Of course, whoever got in on Friday night may have found whatever it was he was looking for. Has there been any sign of disturbance since?'

20

'No, as far as I could see this morning,' said Miss Emily. 'And I went very carefully round all the windows and doors on Saturday night as you can imagine. I even put a piece of stamp edging across the door of the library at the top where no one would be likely to notice it, and it was still there this morning.'

Miss Hogg looked at her admiringly.

'We must hope they haven't yet found it, whatever it was, and I will come up this afternoon. I could stay tonight, but tomorrow I may have a friend coming to stay with me.'

And half an hour ago, she reflected, she was doubting whether she would ever have any clients.

Miss Emily coughed.

'There is just the matter of fees,' she said. 'I expect you have some sort of tariff for these things.'

'Two guineas a day and expenses,' said Miss Hogg, who had never until that moment given it a thought. 'Of course as you live so near there won't be many expenses, in fact I should think there'll hardly be any at all. It's only if I have to shadow people, and take taxis and trains and things,' she added grandly, as if her life were one round of leaping into taxis, and catching boat-trains by the skin of her teeth.

'I quite understand,' said Miss Emily. 'It seems very reasonable and I will give you a cheque for the first week this afternoon.' She got up and held out her hand. 'Thank you, Miss Hogg. I'm so glad I noticed your plate. It's relieved my mind very much to put the problem into other and more competent hands. One doesn't like to think of intruders making free of one's house while one is asleep.'

'Hogg,' Miss Hogg admonished herself, as Miss Emily turned into Acacia Avenue and went on towards the village, 'this is your first case, and you've got to make a success of it.' She stood still in the hall, took off her pince-nez and polished them vigorously. 'But what the hell,' she asked herself, 'is it all about?'

CHAPTER 4

At one o'clock exactly Miss Hogg entered the Reference Room of the South Green Public Library armed with an imposing note-book, stamped with the royal arms on the cover (it had been supplied to the Superintendent some years before), a fountain-pen, a ball-pen, and a BB pencil. Most of her time she spent poring over various volumes of the *Encyclopaedia Britannica*. From the library she took a short cut into Barbrook Drive and so to the West Side of the Green, and was entering the gate of the Laurels as the church clock struck three. She felt a pleasant sense of importance but also, it must be admitted, a slight sinking feeling in the pit of the stomach.

The middle-aged woman who answered the door, in a dark blue dress with a small lace apron, was obviously Phyllis Maud. Miss Hogg was momentarily taken aback. She had been picturing a girl straight from school.

'I think Miss Dewdney is expecting me,' she said.

'That's right, miss,' said Phyllis Maud. 'You're the detective, miss, aren't you?'

The slightly scared feeling vanished away. Miss Hogg felt completely herself again.

'I am,' she said. 'I suppose you've no ideas at all about what has been happening?'

'I haven't indeed, miss.' They were standing in the hall, a gloomy prelude to the house proper, with a tessellated floor, and a stained-glass window in red and blue and green and yellow half-way up the Victorian staircase. Phyllis Maud glanced up the stairs, and then lowered her voice to a conspiratorial whisper. 'I did think Miss Emily was imagining things, but that nice young man who writes in the *Glamour Girl* and the *Sunday Clarion*, he's been here for the last fortnight, and he's quite in a taking as well. He's in the library now, miss.'

'Then I'd better go to the library,' said Miss Hogg. 'If you will show me the way, then you can tell Miss Emily I've arrived.'

The library was a long, high, rectangular room occupying almost all the back of the house facing the garden. It was entered from a short passage under the stairs, the passage ending in a glass-panelled door which opened on to the garden. The door by which she entered was in one of the shorter sides, books lined the longer wall to her left, and opposite were three french windows. The walls were distempered a dull crimson, and in niches some three-quarters of the way up were busts of ancient worthies. Miss Hogg was able to recognize Socrates and Julius Caesar. Just on the right of the door was the mummy-case, the swathed figure and painted mask looking oddly out of place, and beyond the mummy-case was the roll-top desk which was very like the one that was now Miss Hogg's. In between the windows were the cabinets, one of which she had already heard about, and two very large mahogany tables, loaded with papers and books, occupied a good deal of the central floor space. In the middle of the wall on the opposite side from the door was the fireplace, an old-fashioned steel grate in a setting of Purbeck marble, surrounded by a brass fender with a massive array of brass shovels and tongs and pokers In the angle of the wall between the fireplace and the extreme left-hand window was piled a variety of old leather and japanned tin trunks and several wooden packing-cases. Kneeling in front of one of these as they entered, and partly obscured by one of the leather arm-chairs at the side of the fireplace, was a man who looked young in the distance, but as Miss Hogg walked over to him she realized he must be her own age if not older. She had once attended a series of lectures he had given in the church hall on 'The English Romantics', under the auspices of the W.E.A., but that was the year the war ended, and he could hardly be expected to remember her.

She underestimated Mr. Bartley Craig. His success was founded on industry. He could produce whimsical paragraphs about his cat, or his housekeeper, or the roses lining his garden path with the ease and facility of a sausage machine, but his years of practice had been as laborious as those of any other virtuoso. And his card-index of fans, correspondents, acquaintances and persons casually encountered was kept as meticulously as any ledger in the Bank of England. As soon as he had heard from Miss Emily that she had consulted Miss Hogg he had slipped round the corner to his own house, looked up the fan-mail index, drawn a blank, and then remembered the lists of those who had attended his South Green course of lectures. There she was, with a dagger at the side which was his private symbol for 'dull', and now here he was, primed for their encounter.

Swiftly he dropped the lid of the wooden box in which he had been rummaging, and if a faint scowl had momentarily crossed his face, there was no trace of it left as he jumped gracefully to his feet, and came forward with a plump hand outstretched, turning on charm as one might turn on a tap.

'Miss Hogg,' he said. 'How nice to see you. I don't expect you remember me, but you came to my lectures all those years ago.'

'Only five years ago.' There was something in Miss Hogg's ancestry that was antipathetic to charm.

'Is it only five? It seems ages and ages ago. Just at the end of that dreary war.'

Bartley Craig had spent the first two years of the war in the Ministry of Information, having got in on the ground floor through a friend who was a great friend of the secretary of a Cabinet Minister, and the remainder of the time in the Propaganda Department of the B.B.C. His evenings had alternated between the *Abri du Ritz* and a cottage in Berkshire, except for a devastating two months in Manchester which had nearly brought on a nervous breakdown.

'I should like to get a clear picture of what has been happening,' said Miss Hogg. She was still carrying the note-book with the royal arms on the cover.

'My dear, there's nothing clear about it. It might just be a cat.' He waved a hand towards the leather arm-chairs by the fireplace. 'Won't you sit down?'

Although the disposition of the room had remained almost unchanged for at least a hundred years, it had at some time been wired for electricity, and a two-bar electric fire was glowing just inside the brass fender and in front of the steel grate.

'Tell me about the note-book,' said Miss Hogg, flipping over the pages of her own. It struck her as she settled into one of the arm-chairs that she was more entitled to play the host than Mr. Bartley Craig for she was at least staying in the house.

'There's nothing really to tell. It just disappeared.'

'What I want to get at is what exactly it was. Was it one of your note-books, or was it one of Sir Arthur's? You see, there must be some reason for its disappearance.'

Mr. Bartley Craig did not answer immediately. He walked over to the middle window, his hands in his pockets, looked out into the garden, and then strolled back to the fireplace.

'It was one of Sir Arthur's note-books,' he said.

'What was in it?'

'It was just jottings he had made on his last journey.'

'Armenia, wasn't it?'

25

'Transcaucasia – Azerbaijan I believe they call it nowadays. It was then under the Russian Imperial Government.'

'What was he doing there?'

'Searching for manuscripts, dear. There's a Monophysite colony there, or used to be, complete with monasteries and things. That was the sort of thing he liked. Not my cup of tea at all.'

'Had you read the note-book?'

'I'd only just glanced at it. It was in one of the boxes over there.' He nodded towards the pile of trunks and boxes which were behind the chair in which Miss Hogg was sitting. 'His effects, as I think you call them, were sent back a year or two after he died by our ambassador in St. Petersburg.'

'You say Sir Arthur or, rather, his manuscripts, aren't your cup of tea,' said Miss Hogg, looking at him speculatively. 'Then what made you suddenly decide to write a life of him?'

For an instant the middle-aged babyish face looked positively malignant.

'Why shouldn't I? Do you think I'm not capable, dear?'

'What I'm trying to get at,' replied Miss Hogg patiently, 'is what has made Sir Arthur so popular suddenly. He's been dead nearly a century, and now, suddenly, there's you, and Sir Wellington Orde, and that American professor, all tumbling over each other to get out a life of him.'

'I don't know anything about the Orde person, or the American if it comes to that. I think it's very mean of them poaching on what are, after all, my preserves.'

'I should have thought they were Miss Emily's.'

'Oh, you know what I mean.' Bartley Craig got up again and went over to the window. 'The Victorians are in the news again.'

'Rubbish!' Miss Hogg was at her most schoolmarmish. 'Strachey went out before the war.'

'You must just take it then that there's a vogue.'

'Vogue my foot!' Miss Hogg also got out of her chair, and walked over to the right-hand cabinet. One of the glass doors was partly open, and, hanging from the knob, was a shiny black note-book fastened to a piece of green blind cord.

'I suppose this was the cabinet that had been interfered with?'

Bartley Craig came over and stood at her side.

'Have you your finger-print apparatus with you, dear? I should so adore to watch you go into action.'

'Finger-prints are only useful if the person making them is a known criminal whose finger-prints have been recorded,' said Miss Hogg didactically. 'Has anything been removed, do you know?'

'I don't think so, but I haven't checked with the catalogue. Does there look to be a thing that anyone would want?' He put his hand into the cabinet and brought out a small terra-cotta figure. 'Too repulsive, dear, don't you think?' He put it back, and clapped his hands together to get rid of the wholly imaginary dust.

'Do you know anything about them?'

'Enough to know they aren't really valuable,' said Bartley Craig. 'Besides, it wasn't anything Etruscan they were after.'

'How do you know?' But Miss Hogg's query remained unanswered, for the library door had opened, and Miss Emily came in, followed by a man with sharp features and his hair cut so that it stood on end. He was holding a grey Homburg hat, and Miss Hogg noticed that his feet were encased in shoes of brown and white leather.

'This is Professor Hoade,' said Miss Emily. 'Miss Hogg, who is staying with me for a few days, and Mr. Bartley Craig.'

Professor Amos T. Hoade had that air of assurance which was once the hall-mark of the Bradford millionaire, but which crossed the Atlantic more than a decade ago when the Golden Calf found a new Sinai in Fort Knox. As if distributing largesse in dollars, Professor Hoade came forward radiating goodwill.

'Miss Hogg,' he said. 'A real, live private detective. And Mr. Bartley Craig, the famous writer.'

It was the sure way to Mr. Bartley Craig's heart. Miss Hogg bowed a little stiffly, but Mr. Bartley Craig took the outstretched hand and wrung it with a will.

'I adore America,' he said. 'So big and vital.'

'You know the States?'

'I had a month there before the wretched war, and wrote a book about it, *The Land of Uncle Sam*. It went into three editions, and would have gone into a lot more if the war hadn't come.'

'That's fine,' said the Professor. He turned to Miss Hogg.

'Miss Dewdney has been telling me about the mystery. What's been going on here?'

'I still think it might have been the cat,' said Mr. Bartley Craig, a little too quickly, and quite unconvincingly.

'It certainly wasn't Sarah,' exclaimed Miss Emily. 'She's being far too maternal this week.'

'She's hardly likely to have removed a note-book,' put in Miss Hogg dryly.

'A note-book.' Professor Hoade took her up sharply. 'What sort of note-book?'

'It was one of Sir Arthur Dewdney's, or so Mr. Bartley Craig says, sent back after he died.'

'That's very interesting,' said Professor Hoade. 'He died somewhere in the East, didn't he?'

'At a place that used to be called Chusk, but is now called Ilyagrad.' Bartley Craig looked a little put out. 'Miss Emily tells me that you are thinking of writing a life of Sir Arthur.'

28

'Oh, nothing so formal as that. A monograph, or something of the sort, linked with the present draining of the Pontine Marshes.'

'Then you aren't interested in the later stuff?'

The Professor gave him a quick glance. It struck Miss Hogg that she would not like to have him for an enemy.

'Only in so far as one needs to round off a finished life with a death. He can't be left like Mahomet's coffin.' He turned and bowed to Miss Emily. 'Forgive me, dear lady, for speaking of your revered father in this way. It is impossible to think of one who died while Disraeli was Prime Minister as your father.'

'He died in the year of Sedan,' said Miss Emily. 'I am afraid,' she added, 'that the French have never recovered from Napoleon III.'

'You are a Bourbon?' enquired the Professor delightedly.

'Naturally,' said Miss Emily.

Mr. Bartley Craig had been listening to this exchange with growing impatience.

'Do you know anything about old manuscripts?' he asked. The question might have appeared rude, but Miss Hogg sensed an urgency underlying it.

'*C'est mon métier*,' replied Professor Hoade. He took a wallet from his inside breast-pocket and extracted a card. It was a replica of the one Miss Hogg had already seen. 'I am, in my small way, a palaeographer.'

'Oh,' said Bartley Craig. He had glanced at the card, but did not take it. The Professor put it back in his wallet. 'Perhaps we could sort them out together.'

'I am always glad of expert help,' said the Professor, rather nastily, Miss Hogg could not help thinking. He made a gesture towards the pile of boxes in the far corner of the room. 'If those are all full it is going to be a formidable task.'

This proved to be Miss Emily's cue. 'I will leave you,' she said. 'Miss Hogg, perhaps you will come up and have a cup of tea with me. If anyone else cares for tea, we shall be in the drawing-room on the first floor.'

CHAPTER 5

THE BISHOP of Tucson arrived at the Vicarage in a Daimler hire just after half past five. Mr. Earwicker had been unable to settle down to anything for the last hour; even the phrases in a letter to the *Church Leader* on the burning question of angels on marble tombstones had refused to flow from his pen. He had spent the time perambulating from his study to the hall, and from the hall to the drawing-room in a flurry of anticipation. He had had occasion to ring up a neighbouring Vicar in the course of the afternoon, and had inserted into the conversation, which was on the subject of the Archdeacon's Visitation and Admission of Churchwardens, due to take place the following week, the information that the Bishop of Tucson was staying with him for a couple of nights. 'Wherever is that?' asked his irreverent friend. 'In the Cannibal Islands?' 'Arizona,' Mr. Earwicker answered coldly. 'Same thing almost,' his friend had replied. But it had suddenly struck Mr. Earwicker that he had no idea whether you addressed American bishops as 'My Lord Bishop', or, less correctly, as 'My Lord', or not. He had once heard it argued that only those bishops who were peers of Parliament were entitled to 'My Lord', but a High Anglican worthy who was present had roundly asserted that all bishops were Lords, and that the title came from the Latin *dominus*. Another clergyman present, equally erudite, had maintained that all the clergy, if graduates of their university, were correctly described as *dominus*. Unfortunately, Mr. Earwicker could not remember where the argument had finally led, and what conclusion, if any, they had arrived at. A factor in the present case which had not entered the discussion was that Americans did not believe in Lords, at least in theory, even if their daughters married

31

them in practice. It would probably be better, he thought, to stick to plain 'Bishop'.

As the car drew up at the Vicarage gate the Vicar, who was in the hall, flung open the front door and advanced down the steps.

'How do you do, Bishop,' he said.

Although in ecclesiastical garb or, at least, a black suit surmounted by a clerical collar fitted on to a purple stock, the bishop looked every inch an American. The particular quality is indescribable, but it is compounded of childishness, self-assurance and astuteness, with an overall ruthlessness which can ignore any point of view but its own.

'A nice place you've got here,' said the bishop.

The accent was very American indeed.

'We think South Green is very pleasantly situated,' said the Vicar. 'The advantages of the town with the amenities of the country. Let me take your bag.' The bishop had extracted a large and opulent-looking pigskin suit-case from the depths of the car.

'Thanks. Sure you can manage me for two nights?'

'Of course, of course. Only too delighted.'

'Well, I guess I'll ask this fellow to come back for me on Wednesday. I certainly get lost in your toobs.'

The return of the Daimler having been satisfactorily arranged, they mounted the steps of the porch and entered the hall.

'My dear,' the Vicar said, raising his voice and directing it towards a door on the farther side, 'the bishop has arrived.'

Mrs. Earwicker came out from the door, which was the one that led to the kitchen premises. Her face was flushed, whether from the exertion of making a rabbit pie or a trifle was not clear, though there was a patch of flour on her right cheek, and she had the strained look of one who has found inanimate objects unexpectedly recalcitrant.

'How do you do!' she said. 'It's difficult to get girls these days, so I have to do the cooking myself.'

'That's wonderful!' exclaimed the bishop.

'It doesn't leave you much time for anything else,' said Mrs. Earwicker.

'The bishop is in the Pink Room, my dear?' enquired the Vicar. Considering that he had three times looked into the room in the course of the afternoon to assure himself that everything was as it should be, this was a somewhat unnecessary enquiry. Mrs. Earwicker nodded, and asked them to excuse her. A hissing sound smote the ear as she opened the door giving on the back regions. The sound receded as the door closed behind her. Mr. Earwicker asked the bishop to follow him upstairs.

'This is your room,' said the Vicar, throwing open the door of the Pink Room, and standing on one side to allow the bishop to precede him. The name obviously derived from the peculiarly revolting shade of distemper which had been used on the walls. It has to be said, in fairness to the Vicar, that it dated from a previous incumbency. 'I hope there's everything you want.'

The bishop glanced round, at the large brass bedstead, the solid mahogany wardrobe and chest of drawers, the marble-topped washstand, the mahogany towel-rail, and the two cane-bottomed chairs.

'Everything,' he said.

'I'll just show you the geography of the house,' said Mr. Earwicker, 'and then you can come down to the study when you're ready. I thought you'd like a quiet evening this evening.' The Vicar spoke as if the bishop had that moment crossed the Atlantic. 'We haven't asked anyone in to supper, but a Mrs. Vessey is coming in to coffee afterwards, and if you play bridge, she would make up a four. Mrs. Vessey is an American,' he added.

'Mrs. Vessey,' echoed the bishop sharply. He had been opening his pigskin suit-case, but he turned and positively glared at Mr. Earwicker. 'What State does she come from?'

'I'm afraid I've no idea.' The Vicar was a little taken aback. 'It's not the sort of thing I've ever thought of asking her. And, of course, she's English now. Her husband is quite a famous artist, but he's rather an invalid, and never goes out. They have a modernized cottage just off the Green.'

'I avoid Americans when I'm on holiday,' said the bishop. As if conscious that he was being a little ungracious he broke into a laugh. 'There are few places on this little old globe where you won't find some of us today. And I like a game of bridge.'

In the study the Vicar tried to steer the conversation towards the subject of preaching in the United States, but with little success. The bishop seemed to wish to avoid ecclesiastical subjects. When he did venture into the field the Vicar could only imagine that he was joking.

'I sure enjoyed your letter about aumbries,' he remarked on one occasion.

'You have Reservation in the States?' enquired the Vicar.

'All our seats are free,' replied the bishop.

Was it an obscure joke, the Vicar wondered, or a plain *non sequitur* due to the bishop's hardness of hearing. That he must be a little deaf seemed plain when the Vicar had twice asked him questions about his diocese, and the bishop had countered with questions which bore no relation to the subject.

'Chicago is a great little town,' remarked the bishop on another occasion. The Vicar, whose knowledge of America was not extensive, and whose mind connected Chicago only with gangsters, looked astonished.

'Its situation,' said the bishop, as if sensing the other's disapproval. 'I have a brother in Milwaukee.'

'We have another American living on the Green,' said the Vicar, in a rather desperate endeavour to keep some sort of conversation going. 'Rumour has it that he comes from Chicago, but I've never met him. He keeps very much to himself.'

'You seem to have quite a colony,' said the bishop. 'What's the guy's name?'

'Shumacher. He settled here just after the war. I called on him when he first came to the parish, but the manservant said he was not at home, and he never troubled to return the call, so I did nothing more about him.'

A very odd manservant, the Vicar remembered. At some time he had sustained a broken nose and, on the occasion of the Vicar's call he had definitely not been shaved, although it was past three o'clock in the afternoon.

'Shumacher,' said the bishop, and there was another long silence.

'I wonder if you would care to see the church before supper,' suggested the Vicar at last. 'It has some interesting features, and one of the windows is by Comper.'

'Comper, eh?' The bishop got to his feet with alacrity. 'Sure, sure. I just feel like some exercise.'

'I think a coat,' said the Vicar. 'These spring evenings can be very treacherous.'

They strolled up Barbrook Drive, the Vicar raising his hat to one or two parishioners hurrying home from their offices in the city and receiving a greeting in return, and came on to the Green.

'If we walk round the Green by the North Side and come back by the South you will have seen it all,' remarked the Vicar. 'This is the house of Mr. Bartley Craig, the writer. And just beyond is Miss Emily's – Miss Emily Dewdney, I should say.'

The bishop had stopped and was gazing up the drive of

the Laurels.

'Say, haven't I heard of this Sir Dewdney?' he asked.

'Sir Arthur,' corrected the Vicar, looking at him a little askance. 'He has been dead a long time – more than twenty years before I was born – but he was famous in his day.'

'Manuscripts, wasn't it?'

'Towards the latter end. He began as an epigraphist.'

'Did he now!' The bishop seemed hardly to be listening. 'I should very much like to see his library.'

'We will pay a call on Miss Emily in the morning,' said the Vicar. 'She leads rather a lonely life now that her sister is dead, and she is always glad to receive visitors.'

'Too late for paying a call now, is it?'

Before the Vicar could make any reply they were aware of a square figure in somewhat shapeless tweeds coming down the drive. The setting sun flashed a sudden light from her rimless pince-nez. The Vicar raised his hat.

'How do you do, Miss Hogg,' he said. 'May I introduce the Bishop of Tucson. Miss Hogg's father,' he added, turning to the bishop, 'was for many years one of our sidesmen at the church.'

'I was reading a life of Sir Arthur Dewdney just before I left the States,' observed the bishop, ignoring this gambit. 'I was just telling the Vicar here I should like to have a look at his library.'

'You'll soon have to be queueing up,' said Miss Hogg. 'There seems to be a vogue for Sir Arthur at the moment.'

'What do you mean?' asked the bishop sharply.

Miss Hogg glanced up at him in surprise.

'Oh, there's Bartley Craig, he says he's writing a life of Sir Arthur. And there's Sir Wellington Orde – he's there now – and a Professor Hoade from some American University.'

'American!' exclaimed the bishop. 'What do you know!'

'To reply with an American idiom, South Green is lousy with them,' said Miss Hogg with a cheerful grin.

The Vicar's face registered a pained disapproval.

'This is Mrs. Vessey coming along now,' he said. She had just got off a bus at the north-west corner of the Green, which the main London road crossed diagonally, and was walking down to her cottage which was on a footpath leading from the East Side of the Green just below Barbrook Drive.

The bishop swung round as the Vicar prepared to raise his hat.

Mrs. Vessey pattered towards them on high-heeled patent shoes, carrying a Fuller's cake in a white cardboard carton. As she drew near she suddenly faltered, put her hand out to the railings which ran along the front of the Laurels, and crumpled up into a little heap on the pavement.

'Goodness gracious!' exclaimed Miss Hogg.

'Dear me!' exclaimed the Vicar.

The bishop remained speechless.

The Vicar and Miss Hogg moved quickly forward. Already Mrs. Vessey was coming round, and trying to raise herself.

'It's my heart,' she said. 'Silly of me, but it just gives out sometimes.'

'My dear lady,' said the Vicar. 'Shall I get a chair from Miss Emily's?'

'Oh, no. Please not. I'm quite all right.' Mrs. Vessey struggled to her feet with the help of Miss Hogg's arm. 'It's the most idiotic thing.' The Vicar retrieved the cardboard carton, dented a little at one side, and gave it to her.

'Er, this is the Bishop of Tucson,' he said.

'Oh!' Mrs. Vessey was not yet her social self.

'You were going to come in to bridge tonight, but I'm afraid we can hardly expect you now.' The Vicar had been passing in review through his mind the somewhat limited possibilities of entertainment provided by South Green.

'I'm sorry. I think I'll just go home and go to bed. I'm so sorry.'

'Please don't disturb yourself,' said the Vicar. 'Shall we walk back with you?'

'Oh, no, no, no!' Mrs. Vessey's voice rose to an almost hysterical wail. Without another glance at them she pattered off homewards, leaving an uncomfortable group by the railings of the Laurels.

'I suppose you wouldn't care for a game of bridge this evening?' the Vicar asked Miss Hogg.

'I'm afraid I couldn't manage it tonight. I've started in business on my own today, Vicar, and landed my first job.'

'Indeed,' said the Vicar. 'You are no longer teaching then?'

'No, I'm a Private Investigator, and Miss Emily has asked me to look after her library. Something very odd has been going on there.' She caught the bishop's eye, surprising an emotion which she was unable to classify. 'I have to be back for dinner, and I'm staying the night. Good evening.'

CHAPTER 6

Monday night was uneventful. Until the early hours of Tuesday morning, Miss Hogg was engaged in the library of the Laurels, more or less in the role of a watchdog. In order to pass the time she tried to undertake a little research. She began by taking out the books, one by one, to see if there were anything slipped in between the leaves, but after tackling three shelves and realizing that there were quite a hundred more, she gave it up. Even with both bars of the electric fire on it was chilly in the farther reaches of the library, so after a desultory inspection of the two cabinets, which seemed to contain nothing of any importance from the point of view of a burglar, she dragged one of the boxes that had come back from Armenia – or Azerbaijan, if Bartley Craig were to be trusted – up to the fireplace and began to go through it methodically. What odd things, she reflected, men gave their lives for! Marvell's lines which she had memorized in her training year ('The Augustan Age in Eng. Lit.') came to her lips, and she found herself repeating:

> *How vainly men themselves amaze*
> *To win the palm, the oak, or bays . . .*

. . .

The best thing to do with some of these parchments, she thought to herself, would be to convert them into lampshades. The stands could be those sort of whisky bottles that have bulges in them. A package done up in stained calico caught her eye. Undoubtedly it had been disturbed recently. The outer layer was brown with age, but the present folds did not correspond with the discoloured lines. Inside was a small leather-bound volume, *Ambarvalia*, by Arthur Hugh

Clough, in the edition of 1849. It had been Sir Arthur Dewdney's light reading on his last expedition. In another package, this time of faded green canvas, she found an old pistol, almost a museum piece. After a time, she dragged another box over. As the church clock struck one, she decided to go to bed.

At the Vicarage, Joan had gone to bed, protesting a little as usual, at nine o'clock, and the others followed an hour later. There had been no bridge, and only the most desultory conversation. Mrs. Earwicker had occupied herself darning socks. The Vicar, who had hoped to discuss homiletics in the United States, and especially the opportunities awaiting a visiting preacher, could scarcely disguise his chagrin.

'I can't understand it,' he grumbled to his wife, when they were safely in the sanctuary of the front double bedroom. 'His letter said particularly that he was in this country to arrange exchange visits, and now he's here I can't get a word out of him about it.'

'He's tired,' said Mrs. Earwicker practically. She had a hairpin in her mouth so that it sounded more like 'fired'. 'You know what bishops are. It's never any good bothering about them.'

The gnomic wisdom of his spouse never failed to irritate Mr. Earwicker, but on this occasion he refrained from comment. Whatever its outcome, it had been an exciting day, especially in anticipation, and he was tired. He knelt to say his prayers.

'Your socks,' Mrs. Earwicker remarked, as he came back to earth, 'need mending. I must get you another pair from the airing cupboard in the morning.'

Mr. Bartley Craig had passed a quiet evening in his cottage, as he was wont to call it, on the corner of Barbrook Drive and North Side. His secretary, a petulant young man lately down from Oxford, with black hair that fell down over his right eye, had been sent to bed early. Usually they went up to London for a party, or a number of cronies would drop in for drinks and to listen with half an ear to the hand-made gramophone whose enormous horn dominated the sitting-room, while they pulled their absent friends to pieces. It was an undergraduate room of twenty years before, raised to the superlative degree, for Bartley Craig at forty-five was still the eternal undergraduate, and over the fireplace was a framed reproduction of *Le Fifeur* that had occupied the same position in his rooms at Oriel a quarter of a century before.

With a box of imitation Turkish Delight on the small table at the side of his chair, Mr. Bartley Craig was reading steadily through a holograph diary. Had Miss Emily been able to look over his shoulder, she would have recognized the angular but very readable script of Sir Arthur Dewdney. It was, indeed, the missing note-book which Mr. Bartley Craig had abstracted on the morning following the disturbances of Friday, a move he had already begun to regret. It had been Sir Arthur's custom to keep a journal on his travels, recording each night everything of interest that had occurred during the previous day. Here and there were lines of verse, for Sir Arthur had been a true Victorian. Bartley Craig passed them over impatiently, imagining them to be Sir Arthur's own compositions.

> *Come home, come home, and where is home for me,*
> *Whose ship is driving o'er the trackless sea?*
> *To the frail bark here plunging on its way,*
> *To the wild waters, shall I turn and say*
> *To the plunging bark, or to the salt sea foam,*
>   *You are my home.*

And towards the end of the volume:

> *Come back; come back, and whither and for what?*
> *To finger idly some old Gordian knot,*
> *Unskilled to sunder, and too weak to cleave,*
> *And with much toil attain to half-believe.*
>   *Come back, come back.*

Miss Hogg, at that very moment wrapping the small leather-bound volume in its covering of faded calico, might have given him the source of the quotations. Mr. Bartley Craig turned to the last page. In writing noticeably shaky, which must have been written during Sir Arthur's last illness, were the lines:

> *Sweet eyes in England, I must flee*
> *Past where the waves last confines be,*
> *Ere your loved smile I cease to see,*
> *Sweet eyes in England, dear to me.*

. . .

Was it his wife he was thinking of, or Miss Emily, or her elder sister, Jane, or all three of them? There was material here for just the sort of intimate and sentimental maunderings at which Mr. Bartley Craig excelled. But he did not even make a note. He turned the page impatiently, and saw that there had been one or two other pages, but that they had been torn out. He flung the book on to the large divan heaped with silken pillows that stood in the middle of the room in place of a more conventional chesterfield, stuffed a piece of Turkish Delight into his mouth, and went over to the window which looked across the garden towards Miss Emily's. Drawing aside the curtain, he saw a shaft of light from the nearer library window shining through the laurels.

'Damn!' he said. And then again, 'Damn!'

After a few moments, he let the curtain fall back into place, switched off the light, and went upstairs. Orlando, his marmalade cat, subject of a hundred paragraphs in the Sunday Press and the women's weeklies, followed him slowly, pretending that his actions and those of his master were in reality entirely independent.

In his study, in a rather more pretentious house than Mr. Bartley Craig's, on the other side of the Green, Sir Wellington Orde was consulting an early edition of the *Encyclopaedia Britannica*, the edition, in fact, to which Dr. Whewell contributed the article on Chinese Music. He was sitting in a leather arm-chair at the side of the Adam fireplace, the index volume open at his feet, and several other volumes piled on the floor at the side of his chair. The study was the only room in the house – it was known as the Duke's House, having at one time been the property of the Duke of Cumberland and housing a succession of his mistresses – whose decoration and arrangement owed nothing to Lady Orde. Elsewhere there were flowered cretonnes and chintzes, and pastel shade carpets which were the devil to keep clean, and imitation candles with pink silk shades, and Hepplewhite chairs, from the Tottenham Court Road, and Dresden shepherdesses in glass cases illuminated by neon strips. Lady Orde's father, Sam Hughes, had been a book-maker, though even in those days, long before the advent of Rodent Operators and Mobile Sanitary Officers, his brass plate, first in Camden Square, Islington, and later in Curzon Street, Mayfair, had borne the words 'Turf Commission Agent'. In Curzon Street he had mixed with the nobs, never being unduly pressing over an account, and luck on the Stock Exchange had helped him into a house in Hyde Park Crescent. Mrs. Hughes had fortunately died while they were still in Islington, for she was a good-natured, common little woman, who would have been quite unable to accommodate herself to the grandeurs of Mayfair. Her daughter, christened Petulia, from a novel by Charles Garvice which her mother had been reading just before her birth, had taken to Mayfair as the proverbial duck to water, and although she had had a number of strictly dishonourable proposals from junior members of the peerage, and even from an Old Harrovian, she had kept her eyes resolutely fixed on the main chance. Why she had determined on Wellington Orde, then Assistant Keeper of Rare Books at the Royal Metropolitan Museum, is probably outside the range of rational conjecture. Although Mr. Orde, as he then was, had a leaning towards an occasional flutter, which was how he first came into contact with Sam Hughes, he was fundamentally the epitome of the middle-class virtues, and it was, perhaps, an unconscious desire for security, a recoil from the rackety gaiety of the twenties to the simpler ideals of her mother, which had led her to the altar with the Assistant Keeper of Rare Books. Two members of the peerage sent silver-plated cocktail-shakers, and the Old Harrovian sent the complete works of Charles Dickens in imitation morocco, which he had obtained as a bargain in the Charing Cross Road. Within six months, the Keeper of Rare Books had died, and Mr. Orde had replaced him, and four years later, on the retirement of the Director, he had been promoted to that exalted position – the highest attainable in that branch of the Civil Service – and created a Knight Bachelor.

The advent of the war had taken some of the sting out of retirement, though Lady Orde had found it hard to relinquish the magnificent house which was the official residence of the Director of the Royal Metropolitan, and even harder to forgo the official entertaining in which she had shone as a hostess. But the years of peace had been even more irksome. South Green, which had seemed a haven during the bombing, had become a stagnant backwater again on the conclusion of hostilities. There was very little petrol, and people did not take kindly to invitations from so far afield. Lady Orde was set on a return to Mayfair, even though Sir Wellington had patiently demonstrated that his pension, though it might pass for wealth in South Green, was quite inadequate to maintain an establishment even north of the Park.

Unfortunately, like others before him, Sir Wellington, who was still very fond of his wife, had turned to speculation, and by the end of 1950 he had irretrievably lost almost the whole of his savings. Mayfair was further off than ever, even as Lady Orde, whose once pretty face now showed the crow's feet at the eye corners, and sharply etched lines from the nostrils to the corners of the mouth, grew more insistent on the necessity of a move. Sir Wellington had begun to explore the possibility of doing some sort of literary work. The Oxford Press had, twenty years before, published his *Incunabula of the English Great Houses*, and his name appeared on several pamphlets published for the Museum. He soon found that authorship is not a profession by which money is made, but has become a sideline for those amateurs of letters who are able to earn a living by some other means or, better still, have no need to earn a living at all. A chance lunch at the Athenaeum, which Sir Wellington now visited but seldom, had at least led to a commission from an old school friend, now a publisher of repute, which promised a certain amount of mental employment even if it should not lead to any great augmentation of his bank balance. He was to write a reasonably popular account of the foundation, rise and growth of the Royal Metropolitan Museum, whose centenary year was rapidly approaching. It was while gathering material for a chapter on the Victorian worthies who had enriched the Museum with their benefactions, that he had come across the name of Sir Arthur Dewdney, and with it a vague recollection of a bequest to the Rare Books department (whose full title was the Department of Incunabula, Rare Books and Ancient Manuscripts), stowed away in one of the vast catacombs of cellars that honeycombed the foundations of the Museum. There were several pages of a Syriac version of the *Didache*, he remembered, and an almost contemporary record of the pilgrimage of some famous woman whose name escaped him, as did the details of her journey, and, of course, pages of uncial versions of the Gospels, and even papyri from the Nile valley, though it was not known how or where Sir Arthur had acquired these, as his journeys did not seem to have embraced any place on the African continent. Indeed it was because of this fact, that their provenance was unknown, that these manuscripts were almost entirely valueless, for Sir Arthur had appended no record of where they had been found, and their texts showed no important deviations from better copies already annotated and on show in the Museum. The present Keeper of Rare Books had been surprised to receive a visit from Sir Wellington Orde, and even more surprised when, after some general gossip about the department, he had asked for permission to go over what had been classified so near to junk as to have escaped evacuation during the late war.

But it was while turning over recent acquisitions in the library of the Athenaeum that Sir Wellington had come across the reference which riveted his attention on to Sir Arthur. An American, an honorary member of the Club, had presented a copy of the life of his grandfather, magnificently produced at the expense of the grandson. The grandfather had been a thorough-going Fundamentalist, but had realized that no version of the Scriptures could be relied upon absolutely except the very first, and if the eternal salvation or damnation of every soul in the world depended on the meticulous observance of every precept in that version, then it was essential that it should be found. Although such Biblical scholars as then existed in America had assured him that no original copy of even a single page of the New Testament had survived from the first century, indeed that hardly anything of any great importance had survived from the first three, he had argued that if the Deity meant the world to be governed by the precepts of a certain work which He had caused to be written down at some definite period of history, that work must be in existence, and must be simply awaiting discovery. Being several times a millionaire, for he had staked a claim to a considerable part of Nevada before the political fortunes of Abraham Lincoln required that it should have conferred upon it the benefits of Statehood, he had been able to finance several expeditions which made laborious but fruitless journeys to Italy, Greece and Syria. At last the old gentleman had himself made the journey to Europe and, by a fortunate chance had been introduced to Sir Arthur Dewdney. Sir Arthur, for whom travel anywhere was even more delight-ful than the achievement of some object at the end of the journey, had gladly fallen in with his patron's wishes, and it was on this last excursion that he had met his death. A letter from Sir Arthur was included in the biography of his patron, written less than a week before he had succumbed to the fever which carried him off, and in it he had hinted at an astonishing discovery which he had made, although he had not yet been able to secure possession of the object, whatever it was, that he had found. The letter, which had travelled down the Black Sea and had eventually been franked by Her Majesty's Consul to the Sublime Porte, reached New York eight months after Sir Arthur's death, and five months after the death of the old gentleman to whom it was addressed. The heirs had been too busy dividing up the territory of the State of Nevada to worry themselves about the fate of a hypothetical manuscript in the wilds of Transcaucasia.

Sir Wellington yawned, marked his place in the volume he had been reading with a folded sheet of paper, and got to his feet. The sheet of paper which he had absent-mindedly utilized as a bookmark was in reality the quarterly statement from his bank, a statement which Sir Wellington had tried to push out of his mind. Most of the figures on it, and all those in the extreme right-hand column, had been recorded with the red ribbon of the machine. After putting a small wire guard in front of what remained of the fire, Sir Wellington went slowly up the stairs to bed.

In the flats on the South Side, Professor Amos T. Hoade was securely tucked up in his Maple's bed. The bedroom window was open at the top, and every now and then a little scurry of wind would gently separate the curtains, and allow a shaft of light from the nearby street lamp to dart across the beige carpet, and fall like a silver bar on the wall to the left of the Professor's bed. The only sound in the flat was that of the Professor's breathing, which occasionally, but ever so delicately, trembled on the verge of a snore.

CHAPTER 7

Miss Hogg was awakened, as the church clock struck eight, by Phyllis Maud, who came into her room with a cup of tea. Indeed it was more than a cup, for on a silver tray covered with a lace cloth was a Crown Derby morning tea-set, complete with sugar-bowl, slop-basin and even a little silver tea-strainer, and accompanying it was a small plate on which reposed two wafer-thin slices of bread and butter.

'If you'd rather have lemon, miss,' said Phyllis Maud, 'Miss Emily said I was to tell you we had one.'

'No thank you,' said Miss Hogg. 'It looks very nice. I shan't want to go home.'

'"East, West, home's best,"' said Phyllis Maud. 'If you have one. I'm a norphan myself.'

Miss Hogg reflected that she, too, might be described as an orphan.

'So am I,' she said.

'But you wasn't brought up in a Norphanage,' said Phyllis Maud, who had been sweeping the hearth, for Miss Hogg had found the remains of a fire in the grate when she had at last gone up to bed. The Victorians had known how to enjoy the blessings of a material civilization. 'It makes a difference being a norphan early.'

'I suppose it does,' said Miss Hogg. Sensible people, she reflected, folding one of the pieces of bread and butter and popping it all into her mouth at once, got married early and started a home of their own.

'Breakfast's at a quarter to nine, miss. Shall I take your things into the bathroom?'

Miss Hogg was not at all sure that her more intimate garments would warrant the critical inspection of even one brought up in a Norphanage.

'Don't bother,' she said. 'I'll manage.'

'Very good, miss.'

It was a pleasant and peaceful beginning to the day. Miss Hogg had no premonition of how different the end was to be. For her to be in bed as late as eight o'clock in the morning was a very rare event. Even on Sundays she was a regular attender at the early service, at which her father, in his capacity as sidesman, had usually taken up the collection. The Superintendent had been a firm believer in the aphorism whose modification by Mr. Thurber probably secures a greater measure of approval today:

Early to rise and early to bed
Makes a man healthy and wealthy and dead.

Before entering the breakfast-room, Miss Hogg made a tour of inspection of the library, and the passage out of which it led. Everything seemed to be in place, exactly as she had left it. She reported this to Miss Emily who was waiting for her at the head of the table.

'I always begin with porridge,' said Miss Emily. 'I can't bear these ridiculous packet things they have nowadays. But you need not join me unless you wish. The kidneys and bacon are on the sideboard.'

Miss Hogg expressed a desire for porridge.

'Milk and sugar is by the porridge bowl. You can't get cream these days. I don't suppose we ever shall get back to normal in my time. Nobody is allowed to have anything now unless everybody can have it, which seems to me a lot of nonsense. If some people want to spend their money on food and some want to spend it on horse-racing, or whatever it is they prefer, I don't see why the Government should interfere.' She turned to the problem of the library. 'You don't suppose that they've found whatever it was they were looking for.'

'It's possible,' said Miss Hogg. 'I don't see how we're to know. The only thing that we actually know to be missing is the note-book, and we've only Mr. Bartley Craig's word for that. Somebody has been through those packing-cases recently, but I expect it was Mr. Bartley Craig.'

'Have you ever read any of his books?' enquired Miss Emily.

'I can't say I have.'

'I put one on my library list some little time ago, as he was a near neighbour. It was the silliest production you could imagine. All about his adventures with the pixies in Cornwall. I can't imagine why anyone should want to read such stuff. Why, in my time even fairy stories were more robust.'

'I always preferred Grimm to Hans Andersen,' remarked Miss Hogg.

'So did I,' agreed Miss Emily. 'And I remember a wonderful story called *Puss Cat Mew*. It would be before your time. However, it takes all sorts to make a world, and Phyllis Maud thinks Mr. Bartley Craig is wonderful.'

After breakfast Miss Hogg walked down to her own house, and she was dusting the office when a telegram arrived from her friend in Tolleshunt Darcy. It said simply:

Arriving after lunch Millicent.

Miss Hogg extracted a pair of sheets and a pillowslip from the bathroom cupboard, made up the spare-room bed, examined the larder with a critical eye while remembering that Milly always brought up some country produce of one sort or another with her, and then walked back to the Laurels. She found that the Vicar had arrived with the Bishop of Tucson, and inevitably they were in the library. Miss Emily was showing the bishop some of the Etruscan pottery.

51

'I read about your father back home in the States,' said the bishop. 'He died quite a long time ago.'

'Just eighty years ago next month,' replied Miss Emily. 'I was only quite small at the time, of course. Sometimes I think I remember him, and then again I'm not sure. He had a very distinctive beard. But my mother told us stories about him, and he seemed to be alive as long as she was. They were very devoted, really, although he used to go on such outlandish journeys.'

'What happened on his last journey?' asked the bishop. 'He went prospecting for some American, didn't he?'

'He was looking for early manuscripts,' said Miss Emily. 'Some of those old Greek monasteries have whole libraries of them, I believe. I'm afraid I have taken very little interest in them. I prefer the pottery. What do you think, Vicar?'

'I agree with you,' said the Vicar, who had been glancing through the Diamond Jubilee number of the *Illustrated London News* which was on one of the central tables. 'I can never read the old writing. It amazes me how they manage to decipher it.'

'Did he make any discoveries?' The bishop brought the conversation back to Sir Arthur's last journey.

'I don't think he could have found anything very important,' Miss Emily answered. 'But of course the American who financed his expedition was dead long before my father's effects arrived back from Armenia. I remember my mother saying that the boxes should be kept as they were for a certain number of years, because the heirs might claim, but they never did.'

The bishop had gone over to inspect the boxes in the corner.

'And these are the boxes?' he asked. 'I suppose they have been properly gone through?'

'My friend here, Miss Hogg, is going through them for

52

me at the moment,' said Miss Emily. 'And Mr. Bartley Craig, the writer, you know, is doing some work here. It's surprising what a lot of interest there seems to be in Sir Arthur after all this time. A fellow-countryman of yours, bishop, a professor, came in only yesterday.'

She crossed over to the fireplace, and pulled an old-fashioned bell-rope.

'Shall we go upstairs and have a glass of Madeira wine? Phyllis Maud makes an excellent seed cake, as the Vicar will tell you.'

'Indeed she does,' agreed the Vicar, abandoning the *Illustrated London News* with alacrity.

'I think I'll stay down here,' said Miss Hogg, as the Vicar held the door open for Miss Emily, and waited for the bishop to follow. 'I want to go through the rest of the boxes.'

She was startled to intercept a brief glance from the bishop. It reminded her of how he had looked at her the previous evening, just after Mrs. Vessey had fainted. But this time there was no ambiguity in his glance. It was a look of quite astonishing malignancy.

For ten minutes she was left in peace, sitting by the electric fire, and doing nothing at all. There was nothing even to speculate about. Sir Arthur might have made some discovery of importance, and some present-day person might be trying to get hold of it, but whether that person had succeeded or not it was quite impossible to determine. 'If they have,' she said to herself, 'we shall just hear no more about it, and nothing more will happen here.'

She was dozing off; for she had had a late night and the somewhat later hour of rising had hardly compensated for it, when she suddenly snapped to attention as the door opened, and Mr. Bartley Craig came into the room.

' Ah, the female sleuth!' he exclaimed rather nastily, or perhaps it was only facetiousness. 'Phyllis Maud told me I should find you here. How apt her name is, don't you think? You look at her, and see the Phyllis, and then, just like shot silk, she dissolves into Maud. You can't imagine one without the other.'

Miss Hogg made no reply to this nonsense. Before she had sat down, she had dragged one of the boxes from the corner up to the fireplace, and now she lifted the lid.

'Are you looking for anything in particular?' asked Bartley Craig.

'Were you?' she asked in return.

'One simply doesn't know what to look for,' said Bartley Craig petulantly. 'I suppose you've no clue?'

'None,' said Miss Hogg. She looked up at him. 'I wish you'd tell me what exactly put you on to Sir Arthur.'

Bartley Craig, his hands in the pockets of his beautiful grey flannel suit, had strolled over to the cabinet from which dangled the catalogue written out nearly a century before by Sir Arthur.

'I'm writing a book about Victorian worthies, dear.'

'Oh, come off it,' said Miss Hogg, in the no-nonsense manner that had stood her in good stead at the County School for Girls.

'All right, don't believe me. I don't see why the hell I shouldn't write a book about Victorian worthies. What's it got to do with you, anyway?'

Miss Hogg was gratified to sense the schoolboy peeping through the layer of sophistication.

'It was you brought me into this,' she said equably, 'by complaining to Miss Emily that someone had been in on Friday night and taken a note-book.'

'Someone had been in,' said Bartley Craig. He came back to the fireplace and flung himself into the arm-chair on the opposite side of the fireplace. 'There wasn't much in the note-book, anyway.'

'You'd read it, then?'

'Oh, yes, I've read it. It was full of poetry the old boy wrote. But the vital pages, if there were any, have been torn out.'

Miss Hogg considered this tense for a moment in silence.

'I wish you would tell me what exactly you are looking for,' she said.

'Oh, do stop this sleuthing business,' exclaimed Bartley Craig crossly. 'I wish I'd never mentioned about the old note-book, or the things being moved. Phyllis Maud probably took it to light the fire with.'

'Rubbish!' Miss Hogg took off her pince-nez and polished them vigorously on her handkerchief. 'Are you trying to find whatever it is for the honour and glory, or were you thinking of making something out of it?'

'My dear good woman!' exclaimed Bartley Craig in tones of outrage.

'Don't good woman me,' said Miss Hogg, clipping on the pince-nez again, and giving him a straight stare through them. 'I wish you'd come off it, and just be honest for once. If it's honour and glory you want, I'm not out to snatch it from you, and Miss Emily is far too old to bother about such nonsense. And if you think you can realize on whatever it is, you must obviously see by now that it's quite out of the question.'

Mr. Bartley Craig looked at her with quite undisguised admiration.

'Portia,' he said. 'I knew you reminded me of somebody. I think you're being very rude,' he added. 'I'm sure I could have you up for libel.'

'Slander,' corrected Miss Hogg. 'But in any case, there's nobody here but ourselves.'

'I suppose,' said Bartley Craig, as if coming to a decision, 'it's honour and glory, as you call it. You have to keep before the public eye all the time, if you're a popular writer, as I am. And if Sir Arthur had made some really shattering discovery just before he died and I rediscovered it, it would help me a lot.'

'Nobody seems to know exactly what he was looking for.'

'Oh, yes they do. He was looking for the earliest known version of the New Testament. For the original, actually. Not that there was any chance whatever of finding it, I'm given to understand, but he might have found a few pages.'

'Then I was right about the *Codex Sinaiticus*! Miss Emily said he wasn't interested in the Christian religion.'

'I don't suppose he was, as such. And until recently I don't think anyone knew what he had been looking for. It was only in January that an American book was published giving the details of his last expedition, and I shouldn't have come across it except for an accident. Someone took me to lunch at the Athenaeum, and left me in the library while he made a phone call.'

'How very odd,' said Miss Hogg.

'It was a university thesis or something of the sort.' Mr. Bartley Craig suddenly leaped out of his chair and clapped his hands. 'Do you know,' he said, 'it's just dawned on me why the Professor's name sounded familiar. I'm an idiot, a double-barrelled idiot.'

'If you say so,' said Miss Hogg. 'Go on.'

'The writer of the book. He was a grandson or a great-nephew of the chappie he was writing about. Do you know what his name was?'

'I've no idea.'

'Silas Hoade.'

'Goodness! Then Amos T. is probably a relation, too.'

'I suppose,' said Bartley Craig, flinging himself back into the arm-chair, 'he could stake a claim to all this junk in these boxes.'

'Hardly, after all these years, unless Miss Emily consented, of course. There must be something like a Statute of Limitations. I remember Miss Emily saying that the boxes had been kept as they were because it was thought the American heirs might make a claim, but they never did. And by that time, I suppose, nobody thought they were worth bothering with. Besides, there must be quite a number of things in them that were personal to Sir Arthur.' She stooped and lifted a folded metal and canvas contraption out of the box at her feet. The canvas was yellow with age where once it had been green, and there was rust on the metal parts. Still attached to it was a card bearing the words:

THOMPSON'S SANITARY CONVENIENCE
For Big Game Hunters, Explorers and Foreign
Travellers. Absolutely invaluable. Entered at
Stationers' Hall
As Supplied to Her Gracious Majesty
Queen Victoria.

'Do you think Queen Victoria ever used one?' asked Bartley Craig.

'Perhaps the plumbing at Balmoral was more primitive than we know about,' said Miss Hogg. 'Or it may have been Osborne.'

There was an interruption. The door opened, and the bishop came in, oozing affability.

'I thought I had left my hat,' he explained, looking round, though not very convincingly. 'A really old-world room.'

'Old world is right,' said Bartley Craig. 'It could do with central heating.'

The Vicar popped his head in at the door.

'I've found your hat,' he said. 'It was in the hall.'

'Thank you,' said the bishop. He turned to Miss Hogg. 'We may meet again. Miss Dewdney has very kindly said I may look over her father's books this afternoon.'

He gave a little bow, and followed the Vicar out of the room.

'What do you know!' exclaimed Miss Hogg, an expression she had picked up from the girls of the County School. 'Another of them!'

CHAPTER 8

Miss Hogg was at home in Acacia Avenue waiting for her friend when Miss Millicent Brown arrived shortly before three o'clock, a plump little figure in a belted mackintosh and an unfashionable hat. Miss Hogg stood a little to one side, so as not to obscure the splendour of the brass plate which she had well and truly polished not an hour before, and she was gratified to hear her friend's exclamation of approval.

'Why, Hogg, I think that's wonderful!' She stopped in the doorway, a canvas holdall in one hand, and a knitting-bag crammed to overflowing in the other, her head, surmounted by the shapeless piece of green felt, bending forward, and beamed approval. She and Miss Hogg had been at school and college together, and remained firm friends, but the difference in their characters was indicated by the fact that whereas Miss Hogg had always remained 'Hogg', her friend was known to everyone as Milly.

'It's just real professional,' said Milly. 'You always did have the brainiest ideas.'

'And I've got a case,' said Miss Hogg, with pardonable pride.

'No! Why, that's just too wonderful.' Milly radiated approval. As if about to confer a prize on a favourite pupil, she dumped the holdall, and fished in the knitting-bag. A brown-paper package fell with a thump to the hall floor.

'I do hope that isn't the eggs – no, it's the butter. I've brought half a pound of butter, Hogg dear, and a dozen eggs, and there's a chicken in the other bag all ready to go into the oven.'

'That's very nice of you, Milly.'

'I read between the lines,' said Milly. 'It seemed to me you wanted cheering up. But, of course, you hadn't got the

59

case when you wrote, and that will have made a difference. You must tell me all about it.'

'As soon as I've made the tea.'

And over the tea Miss Hogg recounted the mysterious affair of the missing note-book, and the moving objects.

'If it wasn't the cat or the maid,' said Milly sensibly, having digested all this, 'it must have been somebody from outside. Is it easy to get in?'

'There's a door into the garden at the end of the passage by the library, and I suppose anyone could get a key made. No, that won't do, because the key is in the door on the inside, and you couldn't get another one into the keyhole for it, or if you did manage to push it out, you couldn't put it back from the outside when you went out. Somebody could have left the catch open on one of the windows, and that would mean it must be someone who had been there during the daytime. As a matter of fact,' she added, 'they're the sort of windows you could easily open with a penknife, but there didn't seem to be any scratches, because I looked.'

'What will you do if nothing more happens?'

'I suppose Miss Emily will call the whole thing off.' Miss Hogg's mouth drooped as she saw her first case vanishing into thin air. 'But there must be something,' she went on, 'or there wouldn't be all these people interested.'

'Unless whoever it was got in on Friday night got the thing they're all looking for,' said Milly, 'and I don't see how you're ever to know.' Her hand hovered over the plate of what the confectioner called mixed fancies, deciding between the rival merits of an éclair and a square cake covered with violet icing. 'You do have the loveliest cakes, Hogg. You used to bring some of these back to Clifton Hill House with you, and we always finished them the same night. It was the one thing that used to take the edge off that awful journey to Bristol.'

'When we've had tea we'll walk round to the Laurels, and I'll introduce you to Miss Emily. She's quite a character. I told her you were coming, and so I shouldn't be staying there tonight. In any case, I don't think there's much point in it.'

'I'd like to meet Bartley Craig,' said Milly, licking her fingers. 'I read him every week in *Woman's Fancy*. Is he as good-looking as his photographs?'

'His hair is receding rather quickly, and he looks quite as old as me,' said the unsentimental Miss Hogg. 'But he dresses very beautifully.'

'You always were rather catty about young men.'

'Young men my foot! Bartley Craig is older than I am.'

'And he looks about twenty in his photographs.' Milly turned for consolation to the plate of fancies. 'But of course I knew he couldn't be.' She took a cake with white icing on it this time, piped with chocolate and surmounted by a glacé cherry. 'They had almost exactly the same photograph of him before the war. It's rather disappointing seeing famous people close to. Do you remember when the Prince of Wales came to Bristol?'

'I was having mumps,' said Miss Hogg. 'If you don't want another cup of tea, we'll stroll round to the Green.'

To Milly's disappointment, Mr. Bartley Craig was not at the Laurels when they arrived, but Sir Wellington Orde was. He gave them a glance of extreme irritation as they entered the library, and then turned his back on them. In his hand was a volume he had taken down from one of the shelves.

Miss Hogg was not in the least deterred.

'Sir Wellington, isn't it?' she asked. 'This is my friend, Miss Brown. I'm staying with Miss Emily at the moment, helping her to go through Sir Arthur's things.'

'How do you do!' said Sir Wellington, as if faintly repelling a bad smell.

'Actually I shan't be staying tonight, as my friend has come up from Essex. But she's going to help me go through the boxes.'

'It is surely a task for an expert,' said Sir Wellington. He replaced the volume he had been looking at, and took down another. 'Parchments and manuscripts can be destroyed only too easily by an amateur.'

'Oh, we shall take the greatest care,' Miss Hogg replied cheerfully. 'Most of them seem quite tough. I was thinking they'd make nice lampshades.'

Sir Wellington recoiled visibly, and gave her a baleful glare through his horn rims.

'Have you any qualifications as a palaeographer?' he asked nastily.

'None,' said Miss Hogg. 'I didn't even know what it was until I looked it up in the library yesterday afternoon. But Professor Hoade has, and he's very eager to give a hand.'

'Is Professor Hoade here – Professor Amos T. Hoade?' Sir Wellington looked really taken aback.

'He's in the flats. By Lord Hounslow's.'

'Surely he would have called on me,' said Sir Wellington, almost as if speaking to himself. 'I had no idea he was in England.' He turned to Miss Hogg, and the antagonism had momentarily vanished, overlaid by some other emotion. 'Have you any idea what he is here for? I mean, is he engaged on some research connected with Sir Arthur?'

'He only came in yesterday for the first time – no, I'm wrong. He called on Miss Emily last week, but yesterday was the first time I saw him. I think he said something about a monograph connected with the Pontine Marshes.'

'Fiddlesticks!' exclaimed Sir Wellington. 'Sir Arthur's Etruscan studies were entirely fruitless, and he abandoned them at least a century ago.'

'I understand from Mr. Bartley Craig,' said Miss Hogg pleasantly, 'that Sir Arthur was trying to find an original copy of the Scriptures.'

'Of the Christian Scriptures,' amended Sir Wellington. 'No such thing exists or has ever existed. Before even the Canon of the New Testament was decided on there only existed copies of copies. The earliest versions were oral, like the Sagas of Iceland.'

'Wouldn't Sir Arthur know that?'

'He was riding a hobby-horse, and he didn't care very much where it led him. In any case, Biblical criticism was not very advanced in this country a hundred years ago. What he was actually looking for, as Professor Hoade well knows –' Sir Wellington broke off and looked at his wristwatch. 'It can be of very little interest to you, young woman,' he said, with a reversion to his earlier manner. 'I have begged Miss Emily to have the contents of these cases submitted to expert scrutiny, and I would gladly give up the time necessary to examine them.'

'Mr. Bartley Craig has been through them once.'

Sir Wellington closed his eyes in an expression of extreme distaste.

'I presume you know that an expert examination of a collection of old manuscripts such as appear to be in those boxes could take months, literally months. The more valuable pieces are almost certain to be palimpsests, and the original writing might be quite invisible to the naked eye. Would you be able to recognize a page of an uncial version of the Gospels if you saw one?'

'I would not,' said Miss Hogg cheerfully. 'Yet,' she added.

'Nor would your young friend, Mr. Bartley Craig, I am sure.'

'He isn't a particular friend of mine,' said Miss Hogg.

Sir Wellington put back the book he was holding, and turned to go.

'Tell me, Sir Wellington,' said Miss Hogg pleasantly. 'Are you in this as a member of the Honour and Glory school, or what?'

'I don't understand you.' Sir Wellington was at his most frigid.

'Bartley Craig admitted that he was.' Miss Hogg was quite unabashed. 'But, of course, there are other possibilities.'

'I think you are an extremely impertinent young woman,' said Sir Wellington, and the room shook as he slammed the library door behind him.

'It's something, Hogg,' said Miss Brown, who all this time had been pretending to study a privately printed *Catalogue of the Antiquities in the Private Museum of the Rt. Honble. the Lord St. Oswald*, 'to be called a young woman at our age.'

CHAPTER 9

TUESDAY was another late night for Miss Hogg. Until close on midnight, she and her friend sat up talking, first over a bottle of white port from the grocer in the Parade, and latterly over a jug of cocoa. 'Just like dear old Clifton Hill House,' said Milly, as she sipped the thick sweet beverage, and listened to Miss Hogg's Italian saga. 'What a tiresome man that Mr. Dalrymple sounds.'

'He is very young,' said Miss Hogg. She could afford to be indulgent in retrospect. 'He just felt he had to be efficient all the time, and it was rather wearing. Americans would probably have appreciated it.'

The mention of Americans brought them back to the mystery of the Laurels, and the part played in it by Professor Amos T. Hoade.

'He's a grandson or a great-nephew of Sir Arthur's patron,' explained Miss Hogg. 'He's probably got a very good idea of what it was Sir Arthur found. He wouldn't take a flat in South Green unless he had some very clear object in view.' She finished her cocoa and looked reflectively at the bottle of white port, but decided against it. 'What I think is that the whole thing turns on that note-book that Bartley Craig says is missing. I wouldn't put it past him to have pinched it himself, but apparently the vital pages have been torn out. That means someone else was there before him.' She took off her pince-nez and polished them vigorously. 'If somebody got at the note-book it must have been done by Thursday night. Up to then, Bartley Craig hadn't realized it was anything special, or perhaps he hadn't discovered it at all. When he does come across it, he realizes it's Sir Arthur's last diary, and decides to take it home. He tells Miss Emily it's missing, partly to cover himself, and partly to arouse suspicion of some unknown. And then he finds someone has already been at the note-book, and torn pages out, and on Saturday he discovers there really has been someone from outside rummaging round the library.'

'You always did have a brain, Hogg,' said Milly, who was listening to her with parted lips.

'Now why was the library disturbed on Friday night?' She paused, but Milly did not attempt to answer, sensing it was a purely rhetorical question. 'Obviously this time they were looking for the actual thing, whatever it was, that Sir Arthur had discovered. So they've either found it, or they haven't,' she concluded rather lamely. 'But if they haven't, they are sure to try again.'

'And then you'll get them,' said Milly.

'Whatever it is must be in those boxes,' said Miss Hogg, ignoring this. 'It seems to me the best thing is to get Miss Emily to have them all locked up safely until they've been properly gone through. And heaven knows who's going to do the job,' she added. 'I wouldn't trust that Sir Wellington Orde an inch, nor Professor Hoade.'

'Do you remember that little man at Bristol Emmie Pargeter was sweet on?' asked Milly. 'He couldn't dance, you remember, and he used to glower from the wall when Emmie was dancing with anyone else.'

'Milly, you're a genius!' exclaimed Miss Hogg. 'He used to go round brass rubbing, and photographing old parish registers. He's the very person we want. And I know where he is, because I noticed his name in the Old Students' List last year. Wait a minute.' She dashed out of the room, and was back in a moment with a small paper booklet. 'Here he is. Greenwood, Alfred. Librarian of the Burghley Library.'

'Does it give the address?'

'No, but everyone knows where the Burghley Library is. It'll be in *Whitaker*.' She was already half-way out of the room again, on her way to the invaluable reference shelf.

'Here it is,' she said on her return, and she read out:

> Burghley Library, St. Stephen's Square, Westminster. Founded 1583. Noted for its collection of Dutch and German incunabula. Open 10 a.m. to 4 p.m. throughout the year, except for Bank Holidays, Good Friday and the month of August. Librarian, Dr. A. Greenwood, M.A, Ph.D.

'Ph.D.!' exclaimed Milly. 'I knew he was brainy. Emmie always said he thought far more about his books than he did about her. I wonder if she married him.'

'You can look through the Old Students' Lists tomorrow,' said Miss Hogg. 'But right now we're going to bed. There's work to be done tomorrow.'

'I'm far too excited to sleep,' said Milly, smothering a prodigious yawn.

It had been a windy night, but the wind was dying down. A gust from the south-west blew the sound of the church clock striking midnight in at Miss Hogg's bedroom window, just as she was climbing into bed. She snapped off the light, snuggled down, and was asleep in a matter of minutes.

Almost immediately, it seemed she was wide awake again. The front door bell was pealing through the house, and every now and then came an agitated knocking.

The disturbance had also awakened Milly.

'What is it, Hogg?' she called, from her bedroom on the other side of the landing.

'Goodness knows,' Miss Hogg shouted back crossly. She was struggling to find the light-switch which hung from the ceiling over the head of the bed, and always evaded the groping hand in emergencies. 'I can't smell fire.'

She found the switch at last, jumped out of bed, put on her dressing-gown and slippers, and proceeded downstairs. The knocking came louder than ever, and reminded her of nothing so much as a performance of *Macbeth* they had given at the County Girls' School the previous Christmas. Miss Brown, huddled in her mackintosh, her hair screwed into some kind of metal curling-pins, watched her from the banister rail. The grandfather's clock in the hall recorded a quarter past one. It was, reflected Miss Hogg, exactly five minutes fast.

At the door when she opened it was an agitated Phyllis Maud.

'Oh, miss,' she said, 'will you come at once, Miss Emily says. There's a man murdered in the library.'

'Goodness!' exclaimed Miss Hogg. She wondered whether it could be Bartley Craig, or Sir Wellington Orde, or even Professor Amos T. Hoade. 'Who is it?'

'Miss Emily thinks it's that bishop who was staying at the Vicarage. And she says, will you telephone to the police. We haven't got the telephone, miss. And please come quick, miss, as I've left her all by herself in the library.'

Miss Hogg had a momentary vision of the intrepid and octogenarian Miss Emily standing at bay between the Egyptian mummy and the roll-top desk.

'I must just slip on a few clothes,' she said. 'I won't be a minute.'

She ought, she knew well, to ring the police immediately, but she was determined to be on the scene before they were. So she quickly dressed, with Milly fluttering round her, and then rang the astonished South Green sergeant just before she left the house with Phyllis Maud. 'I can't tell you any more,' she said. 'The maid has just come round' – this was a white lie at least – 'and I'm on my way there now.'

It was dark and cold as they went up Acacia Avenue and into Barbrook Drive. There was no light in the Vicarage as they hurried past it. The wind had died down, but little eddies stirred the branches of the almond and the cherry trees in the suburban gardens, and sent bits of paper scurrying in the gutter. There was no light in Mr. Bartley Craig's house as they came to the corner, but a beam shone red and blue and yellow from the hall window of the Laurels as they turned in at the drive gate. The front door was ajar, and Miss Hogg pushed it open, Phyllis Maud showing some reluctance to be the first to enter the house. She glanced quickly round, but everything seemed to be as it had always been. With Phyllis Maud at her heels, she made for the library, and went in through the open door.

'Good evening,' said Miss Emily, as if this were a social occasion. 'I am sorry to bring you out at this hour.'

She was sitting by the fire, the brass fire-tongs resting across her knee. She had on a very old-fashioned dressing-gown in faded purple flannel. It had a series of capes descending from the shoulders, reminiscent of a highwayman's coat in the old pictures. But the eye went immediately to the figure behind her, spread-eagled over one of the open packing-cases.

'Are you all right, mum?' asked Phyllis Maud from the doorway.

'I'm perfectly all right. Please wait in the hall, and let the police in when they come. I suppose we ought to inform the Vicarage,' she said, turning to Miss Hogg. 'Or perhaps the police will do that. It will be a shock for Mrs. Earwicker.'

'What was the bishop doing here?'

'I simply cannot understand it. We had gone to bed as usual, and everything seemed quiet. There was certainly nobody down here when I went up to bed because I looked in, and then put the piece of stamp edging across the door.

It was the very last thing I did. And then, less than half an hour ago, I heard a noise. I wasn't asleep – I don't think you need very much sleep at my age though some people say you need more. It must have been the noise of the attack. And almost immediately afterwards I heard the sound of the passage door shutting, the one out there that leads into the garden. You can't mistake it, because the leaded panes of glass are loose, and make a rattling noise. I came down immediately, and found this.' Miss Emily waved the fire-tongs to indicate what was behind her, though studiously refraining from looking round. 'I thought he might be ill, but there's no question about it. Someone has knocked his brains out. And they did it with these,' she added, holding out the tongs.

'Oh, dear,' said Miss Hogg, 'you shouldn't have touched them. Because of the finger-prints,' she explained. She took them from Miss Emily. 'Where were they?'

'Just at the side of the body,' replied Miss Emily. 'Now I come to recollect, that would be the first noise I heard, the man throwing down the fire-tongs.'

Miss Hogg put them down at the side of the body. 'We shall have to explain to the police when they come.' She glanced at the body, and then glanced away. She ought, she knew, to be looking for clues, but at the moment she was feeling rather sick. Perhaps divorce cases offered a pleasanter field after all.

'That far window is slightly open at the bottom,' said Miss Emily. 'I noticed it while I was waiting, because of the draught.'

A murmur of voices from the hall indicated that the police had arrived, and Miss Emily rose to her feet as a man whom Miss Hogg recognized to be Detective-Inspector Bruce of the local C.I.D. came into the room, followed by a uniformed constable.

'Good evening,' he said pleasantly. Miss Emily bowed. His eye fell on the stretched-out form of the bishop. 'Whatever has been going on here?'

'That is what we want you to find out,' said Miss Emily. 'I suppose I should be having hysterics, but curiously enough I remain quite unaffected at the moment. It isn't because I took an instant dislike to this bishop person, but just because the whole thing seems quite unreal.'

'You say this is a bishop?' The inspector looked startled. 'Not London?'

'No, Tucson,' said Miss Hogg. 'It's somewhere in America. He was staying at the Vicarage.'

'If you will excuse me, I should like to go back to bed,' said Miss Emily. 'I am sorry to say, officer, that I picked up those brass fire-tongs. I should have got the poker. It was just that I felt the need of something while Phyllis Maud went to get Miss Hogg. If it has disturbed the finger-prints, as Miss Hogg says, I am sorry, but I am afraid it cannot now be helped. This kind of thing has not happened to me before.'

The inspector looked nonplussed.

'Who discovered the body?' he asked.

'I did,' replied Miss Emily. 'But Miss Hogg knows quite as much about the whole affair as I do. In fact she is investigating it for me – not this murder, of course, but the missing note-book and the moving picture, but I should think this murder is all part of it.'

If the inspector had been given to overt demonstration, he would probably have torn his hair. 'I ought to take your statement,' he said.

'You can take it in the morning,' said Miss Emily. 'It was very inconsiderate of this bishop person to come here to be murdered, even if he was an American. And especially,' she added, 'at this hour of the night.' She turned at the door, which the constable, with a helpless glance at the inspector,

71

had opened for her. 'I have no idea what you have to do in a case like this, but if you would like any refreshments, Miss Hogg, I am sure, will get them for you.'

'My God!' exclaimed the inspector, as the door closed behind her. 'She's nearly a hundred, isn't she?' He dropped on his knees at the side of the body.

'Eighty-three,' said Miss Hogg. 'You couldn't keep her up very well, and she can't possibly have had anything to do with it.'

'Almost anybody could lay a person out with these fire-tongs,' said the inspector, getting to his feet. 'And whatever did she want to pick the things up for? She's dished the only real clue we're likely to find.'

'There may be finger-prints on the window,' suggested Miss Hogg.

'The chap will be here any minute,' said the inspector. 'What did she mean about the cinema and the note-book?'

'It wasn't the cinema, it was a picture that someone took off the wall. I think now it was probably a red herring.' The inspector at this moment came very near to tearing his hair. 'I'd better explain from the beginning. I suppose you've heard that I'm now a private investigator?'

'It was all round the station yesterday evening,' said Inspector Bruce with a grin. 'Good luck, I say, but I don't know what your Dad would have said.'

The Superintendent had believed that the woman's only place was the home, ministering to the comforts of the male of the species, though he had grudgingly allowed that teaching was a less unsuitable profession than most.

Miss Hogg went rapidly over the events of the previous week-end, and gave him the gist of Miss Emily's information of the previous day. The inspector made notes, and was just finishing when Dr. Kershaw who, in addition to having a private practice was also the police surgeon, arrived.

Close on his heels were two other men, all three of them carrying little black bags, who turned out to be the finger-print expert and the photographer. After giving them brief instructions, the inspector turned to Miss Hogg.

'I shall have to go round to the Vicarage,' he said. 'I don't know how Mrs. Earwicker will take it, I've never come across the good lady, but perhaps you'd like to come round with me.'

'Moral support,' said Miss Hogg, accepting with alacrity. They left to the puffing of insufflators and the popping of flash-bulbs. 'That's the part that's quite beyond me.'

'You're all for the little grey cells,' said Inspector Bruce, a trifle rudely, but he had known Miss Hogg for a long time, and his sister had been a pupil at the County Girls' School. 'If you have a brain-wave, I hope you won't hold out on me.'

CHAPTER 10

It was darker and even colder on the Green as they turned out of the drive gate of the Laurels. An economical Council had seen to it that the street lamps were extinguished, and the only artificial light to be seen beneath the cold glimmer of the stars was from the brackets over the three entrances to Ormonde Court on South Side. Over to the north-east was the reflected glow of London but, like the aurora borealis, it seemed only to emphasize the frigid emptiness of the night.

'I suppose it is a manuscript they're after,' said the inspector, turning up his overcoat collar and thrusting his hands deep down into his pockets. 'You don't think he found a gold-mine, or anything like that?'

Miss Hogg reflected for a moment. She had been in too much of a hurry when she left home to bother about gloves, and now she was wishing that she had wasted the extra ten seconds in looking for them.

'I don't know whether there's gold in Transcaucasia or not,' she said. 'Geography was never my strong point. But I think there was a manuscript. Sir Arthur's main object in life was chasing old manuscripts, and Professor Hoade is a palaeographer, and Sir Wellington is in the same sort of line. And the bishop seems to have been interested in the library.'

'He was certainly interested enough to break in – I suppose you noticed the catch on the right-hand window had been forced back. It could have been done with a penknife. The only alternative is that someone else broke in first and he was either an accomplice, or the bishop came upon him unawares, and so he was murdered. But it seems an extraordinary coincidence to me that two complete strangers should suddenly decide to break into Miss Emily's library on the same night.'

'You think, then, the murderer was probably someone whom the bishop knew?'

'At the moment it looks like it. I must say it seems very odd conduct for a bishop.'

'He seemed rather an odd bishop, but then he was an American, and even Anglican bishops aren't what they used to be.'

They had turned down Barbrook Drive, and paused for a moment on the pavement in front of the Vicarage.

'There's the American angle, of course,' said the inspector. 'Shumacher doesn't seem to be in the picture yet, but I shall have to look him up. And from what you say, Professor Hoade is very interested in Sir Arthur.'

'Don't forget Mrs. Vessey.'

'I'd forgotten she was an American. And the point about her is she seems to introduce an element unconnected with manuscripts.'

The inspector pushed open the gate, motioned Miss Hogg through, and ran up the steps to put his finger on the front door bell.

'We don't want to rouse the whole neighbourhood,' he said. 'Though tomorrow I shall have to call at every house and ask if anyone happened to see the old boy leaving the Vicarage.' He stepped back, and looked up at the front of the house, now a merciful grey in hue, and as he did so, a light came on in the hall and the front door opened to reveal the Vicar in a brown woollen dressing-gown. He peered at the inspector, and frowned as he noticed Miss Hogg.

'Whatever is it?' he asked. 'An accident?'

'You have a bishop staying with you?' enquired the inspector.

'The Bishop of Tucson. Surely you cannot want to see

him at this hour of the night. I am aware that the Home Office –'

The inspector interrupted him.

'I'm afraid I have some very unpleasant news for you,' he said. 'The bishop has been found dead in the library of the Laurels.'

'Good gracious me!' exclaimed the Vicar. 'Are you sure? He went to bed soon after ten o'clock.' Conflicting emotions showed their traces in his face, and he clutched his dressing-gown, which was revealing blue-and-white striped pyjamas, with an agitated hand.

'I'm afraid there's no doubt about it. Miss Hogg here has identified him as the person she saw with you early yesterday evening.'

'What a dreadful thing. You had better come in, Inspector. Is Miss Emily hurt?'

'She's very sensibly gone back to bed,' put in Miss Hogg.

'I think we'd better step inside for a moment,' said the inspector.

'Do come in,' cried the Vicar. 'I am really bewildered. Come into the study.'

They followed him into a room on the left-hand side of the front door. It was distempered in maroon, and faded red velvet curtains were drawn across the window which was surmounted by an old-fashioned pelmet. A pedestal desk with drawers down each side was across the corner to the right of the window, in the centre of the floor was a table covered with a red chenille cloth, and on either side of the fireplace was an arm-chair in imitation leather. Across the left-hand wall was a mahogany bookcase with glass doors through which could be seen an array of out-of-date theology and the collected works of various eminent authors. The Vicar huddled himself closer into the dressing-gown and took a chair behind the desk.

'Please sit down,' he said, indicating the arm-chairs.

'I shan't keep you very long,' said the inspector. 'I should just like to look through the bishop's luggage.

'We shall have to try to get in touch with the next of kin. I brought Miss Hogg along because she has been helping Miss Emily, and I thought Mrs. Earwicker might be up.'

'She is awake,' said the Vicar, 'but I hope she will not think it necessary to get up. This will be a great shock to her.' He spoke a little absently, for he had already written off his preaching tour of the United States, and was beginning to wonder about the possible diocesan repercussions of being connected with a murdered bishop. 'It all seems so very uncalled for,' he said.

'Could you tell me what you know about him?' The inspector had taken out his note-book, which he had placed on his knee, while he was holding the fingers of his right hand in the palm of his left in an attempt to restore the arrested circulation.

'Hardly anything.' The Vicar considered for a moment. 'In fact almost nothing.' He opened the top drawer of his desk and extracted a sheet of paper which he got up and handed to the inspector. 'This was the bishop's original letter to me. You will see that he wrote from the Grandiose Hotel in Park Lane. Bless me, that was only on Monday. Until then, Inspector, I had never heard of him.'

'I see,' said the inspector, although plainly he didn't. He glanced through the letter and then handed it to Miss Hogg, almost as if she were his sergeant engaged with him on the case.

'He didn't quite look like a bishop,' said Miss Hogg, glancing across at the Vicar.

'No,' agreed the Vicar, 'he did not. But I imagine that was because he was an American. And his manner may have been inspired by the anticipation of his approaching end.'

Having delivered himself of this somewhat rotund period he relapsed into silence, gazing blankly at the inspector. His own diocesan would probably hold him personally responsible. Bishops were so unreasonable.

'We'd better have a look at his luggage,' said the inspector.

'Certainly.' The Vicar got to his feet and came from behind the desk. 'He was in the Pink Room. If you will come with me, I will show you which it is.' He opened the door and stood aside to let Miss Hogg and the inspector pass through.

They mounted the staircase with its handrail of pitch-pine. The treads were stained a dark chocolate colour, with a worn length of turkey carpet running down the centre. As they reached the landing, Mrs. Earwicker looked out of a door on the right. She was wrapped in what appeared to be an eiderdown.

'Is anything the matter?' she asked.

'It's the bishop, my dear. He's – he's had an accident.'

'Has he?' Mrs. Earwicker's tone indicated that she felt no surprise. 'Don't wake Joan,' she added, and closed the door.

'This is the Pink Room,' said the Vicar, opening a door on the opposite side of the landing, and switching on the light.

Its harsh glare threw into prominence the brass bedstead, the mahogany wardrobe and chest of drawers, the towel-rail and cane-bottomed chairs. It looked singularly uninhabited and cheerless. The bed had been turned down, but had not been slept in, and a small mound betokened the presence of a hot water bottle. On the floor in front of the window was the pigskin suit-case, open. A number of articles were scattered on the floor around it.

'Not very tidy,' said the inspector. He knelt down and went quickly through the contents of the case.

There was a grey suit, a shirt with two collars in a cellophane wrapper, obviously new, two ties, a toothbrush, also in cellophane, an electric razor in a plastic case, copies of the *Saturday Evening Post* and *Life*, and a book which the inspector opened at the title-page, and then handed to Miss Hogg.

'Odd reading for a bishop,' he said, getting to his feet.

The title of the book was *A Text Book of Geology* published by the Oxford University Press.

'There doesn't seem anything more to be done here until the morning,' said the inspector. 'I'd better go back to the station and get on to the Grandiose. He may have left his luggage there, or they may know something about him.'

'What – er – will you do with the body?' asked the Vicar.

The inspector rightly deduced what was worrying Mr. Earwicker.

'Oh, it won't be brought back here,' he said. 'It's probably on the way to the mortuary by now. There'll have to be a P.M. I expect we shall get in touch with some relatives or others very soon. Mostly they seem to have their relatives embalmed and then taken back to the States.'

The Vicar looked relieved.

'I cannot think why this should have happened,' he said gloomily. 'It will cause a lot of unpleasant talk in the parish, and the bishop won't like it at all. It must be very upsetting for Miss Emily,' he added. 'I wonder if I ought to go round and see her.'

'Tomorrow,' said Miss Hogg. 'She's probably fast asleep again by now. These old people are tough.'

'If you are sure,' said the Vicar. 'Then I will call in the morning. But please tell her if you see her first how very distressed I am.'

'Thank you very much for your help,' said the inspector briskly, as they regained the front door. 'I am sorry this should have happened.' He was about to add a bit about beggars can't be choosers, for he was fond of proverbial wisdom, a form of cliché which he rated as highly as Pope did wit, but having examined it, he decided it was unsuitable for the present occasion, and a more apt quotation would not come to mind. 'Good night, sir. I shall have to look in again in the morning.'

CHAPTER 11

Miss Hogg stayed in bed for breakfast on the Wednesday morning, Milly bringing it up for her on a tray at nine o'clock, and as the church clock struck the hour, the inspector turned into the semicircular carriage way which gave on to Sir Wellington's Queen Anne house on West Side. The Grandiose had known nothing of the Bishop of Tucson: he had not been staying in the hotel, he might have lunched there the previous day, on the other hand he might not. They numbered members of the clergy among their clientele, though they let the inspector understand that they were only likely to be upper members of the hierarchy. They had quite a number of American visitors staying in the hotel, and with a weary sigh the inspector had despatched a sergeant to interview them all, and try to ascertain whether one or other of them had entertained the bishop to lunch the previous day.

The inspector stood for a moment looking up at the grey stucco front of the house. Trim and neat, it told him nothing. He had decided to concentrate on the three American residents of South Green, but was calling on Sir Wellington first in the hope that he would have some definite ideas if not actual knowledge of what it was Sir Arthur Dewdney had found in Azerbaijan.

The maid who answered the door, a perky young thing who pretended not to know the inspector although he had been instrumental in getting her sister bound over for shoplifting the previous Christmas, informed him with a toss of her head that Sir Wellington and Lady Orde were at breakfast. He was about to say that he would wait, when a door opened on the hall, and Sir Wellington looked out.

'What is it, Susan?' he asked.

'It's the police, sir,' replied the maid in tones which nicely blended indignation that the police should pester a respectable household, and a smug satisfaction that she at least had done nothing to merit their enquiries.

'Indeed!' Sir Wellington came forward. 'Oh, it's you, Inspector. Good morning. What can I do for you? I've got a licence for the car, and the wireless and Lady Orde's dog, but there's bound to be something one trips up on these days.'

'Good morning, sir.' The inspector made a private note that Sir Wellington looked as if he had passed a sleepless night, and his affability was a little off key. 'I don't know if you've heard yet, but we had a murder on the Green last night.'

'Thank you, Susan,' said Sir Wellington, dismissing the maid. 'Yes, the paper boy told the kitchen staff, and we got it with our morning tea. A dreadful thing. Come in, Inspector, and have some coffee.'

The inspector stepped into the hall. It was a symphony of blue and ivory. On the right, under the stairs, was a Chinese lacquer cabinet, and on the other side, on an ebony pedestal, was an ornamental jar, which, if the inspector had had any knowledge of ceramics, he would have placed somewhere around the time when Shi-Hwang-ti, King of Ts'in, assumed the dignity of Son of Heaven and Emperor of China.

'Nothing for me, thank you, sir,' he said. 'I thought you might be able to give me a little information.'

'I, Inspector!' For a moment Sir Wellington appeared quite taken aback. 'I assure you I had never heard of the man in my life until yesterday.'

'It was information about Sir Arthur Dewdney I wanted, sir.'

'Oh, I see.' Sir Wellington plainly showed signs of relief. 'Come in, come in. You won't mind if I finish my breakfast.'

And he opened the door of the room from which he had emerged, and ushered the inspector in before him.

'This is Inspector Bruce, my dear. He's come about the murder.'

The inspector was surprised to intercept a glance of sheer terror from the lady of the house. Lady Orde, rather heavily made-up, was sitting at a round table in the middle of the room, facing the window, which looked on to the drive. Murder is, the inspector reflected, an unpleasant word, and Sir Wellington had flung it at her somewhat brutally.

'You don't suspect us, do you, Inspector?' Lady Orde gave a little laugh, which tinkled falsely among the teacups. 'Until this morning, I'd never heard of this bishop person.'

'Do sit down,' said Sir Wellington. He took his place at the table again, opposite Lady Orde. In front of him was a boiled egg, from which he had removed the top. A copy of *The Times* was propped against a bowl of flowers in the centre of the table. 'I'm afraid we aren't great church-goers.' He said this as if it plainly absolved them from all connection with the murder.

'I believe you met the bishop yesterday,' said the inspector.

'We didn't actually meet,' replied Sir Wellington sharply. 'I called in at Miss Emily's during the afternoon, and I was given to understand the Vicar had taken him to call there in the morning, but I never actually met him.'

'We know the Vicar, of course,' put in Lady Orde, with another little laugh. 'But only as Vicar. I mean we're not *intimate*. He wouldn't think of bringing any of his visitors in to see us. Even if it was a bishop,' she added.

The inspector ignored this.

'We've been given to understand,' he said, 'that Sir Arthur may have found something of considerable value on his last expedition. I was wondering, sir, if you had any idea

83

what it was. You see,' he explained, as Sir Wellington made a gesture of dissent, 'it seems clear that there was something, and that one or more people have been after it in the last few days. At the moment we've no idea what could have made the bishop want to break into Miss Emily's library.'

'The windows are ridiculously insecure,' said Sir Wellington.

'Oh, it was easy enough,' agreed the inspector, making another mental note, 'but there must have been some quite considerable incentive to make a bishop force an entry in the middle of the night.'

'He may have arranged to meet someone there.'

'His assailant, as you say, may have been someone he knew who was there first and let him in. Equally he may have been surprised by someone who came after. But why I came to see you, Sir Wellington, was that I'd heard you were interested in Sir Arthur's work – you were in the same line yourself I am given to understand – and I thought you might be able to throw some light on what they were after. What is there likely to be of value in Miss Emily's library?'

Sir Wellington put down his egg spoon with a slightly irritated gesture.

'Sir Arthur began as an epigraphist,' he said, in the manner of one beginning a lecture to a learned society, 'but he changed over to palaeography which, as you remarked, Inspector, happens to be my line. I understand that Sir Arthur, on his last expedition, was trying to locate the original version of the New Testament – a thing which he very well knew, even in 1870, had no existence.'

'Surely there must have been something the others were copied from.' The inspector was a little out of his depth, but it seemed to be common sense that copies could not exist unless there had also existed the original from which they were copied.

'You may have heard of the Sagas of Iceland,' said Sir Wellington, in a tone of voice which belied his words. 'They were recited orally for some two hundred years before ever they were actually written down. The New Testament consists of the Gospels, the Acts, the Epistles and the Apocalypse. The Epistles were dictated to an amanuensis except, possibly, for Philemon. The people who received them had copies made, and the copies were passed round and eventually superseded the originals. The Gospels were at first oral – we have it on the authority of Eusebius that Mark, the original of the three synoptic Gospels, was composed from Peter's sermons, and the sayings in Matthew, and the parables in Matthew and Luke were passed on by word of mouth. When at last they came to be written down, the word original would certainly be inaccurate.' Sir Wellington put the tips of his fingers together, and looked over the top of them at the inspector. 'You tend to think in terms of the Book of Common Prayer, of which an original copy exists annexed to an Act of Parliament. But there was no such thing in the early days of the Scriptures. The oldest version we have is on what are called the Chester Beatty papyri, but it is in no sense original. Have I answered your question, Inspector?'

The inspector had been assiduously making notes, but Sir Wellington would have been surprised and chagrined if he could have looked over the note-book. The first three lines ran:

Sir W. up all night?
Lady O. frightened. Of what?
Window.

'Thank you, yes. What did Miss Emily's visitors expect to find then?'

'It is impossible to say.' Sir Wellington abandoned his egg, picked up his coffee-cup and went over to the fireplace. 'Professor Hoade might be able to tell you.'

'Professor Hoade?'

'Amos T. Hoade. He's taken one of the flats for a year, so I was told yesterday.'

'But what is the connection between Professor Hoade and Sir Arthur Dewdney?'

'Professor Amos T. Hoade,' said Sir Wellington, 'is a palaeographer of some repute in America. He is also the great-nephew of Sir Arthur's patron, the person who financed his last expedition.'

'I see,' said the inspector. He closed his note-book and put it back in his pocket. 'Thank you very much, Sir Wellington. I think I'll go across and see this Professor Hoade. He lives in the flats, you say?'

'Next door to Lord Hounslow.'

'Just so.' The inspector got to his feet. 'I'm sorry to have interrupted your ladyship's breakfast, but these things won't wait.'

'It's been quite fascinating,' said Lady Orde. 'I do hope you're successful.'

'It's the first murder we've ever had in this area,' said the inspector. 'Since we were incorporated in the Metropolitan Police at any rate. And the Superintendent doesn't like it.'

'I don't imagine any of the residents will appreciate it very much,' said Sir Wellington dryly. He accompanied the inspector to the door. 'If I can be of any further assistance to you, you must let me know. But I'm afraid this bishop person was an absolute stranger to me.'

CHAPTER 12

THE inspector stood for a moment in the roadway outside Sir Wellington's gate, and glanced at his note-book. It hardly seemed likely that Sir Wellington could have any direct connection with the murder. But, according to Miss Hogg, there were valuable manuscripts in the library of the Laurels, even if Sir Wellington did try to give the contrary impression, and that in itself was suspicious for Sir Wellington was an expert in the subject. In the small hours the inspector had consulted all the reference books available, though he had got a little bogged down with J and E, and why the Pentateuch should really be the Hexateuch. But he knew all about the *Codex Sinaiticus*, and the *Codex Bezae*, and the *Codex Vaticanus*, though he would scarcely have been able to answer an examination question on the *Peshitta*. It was known, in the undefinable way that these things are known, that Sir Wellington was very hard up. On the first page of his note-book the inspector had written down a provisional list of suspects, some of them, indeed, hardly suspects but persons he intended to interview. The name of Sir Wellington Orde was at the head of the list. He would have liked to put a line through it, but instead he simply inscribed after it a question mark. Having done this and put his note-book away again, he walked to the south-west corner of the Green where there was a blue police telephone kiosk, and rang through to the station. Nothing, he was informed, had come in, and there was no news yet from the sergeant. He informed the constable who was operating the switchboard that he was proceeding to the flats to interview Professor Hoade, and that from there he would go on to the Vesseys.

The flats – their actual name was Ormonde Court –

dominated South Side, standing four stories high behind a small courtyard which served as a car park for the residents. The building had that neo-Georgian look reminiscent of so many of the inter-war extensions to the Cambridge Colleges, a hint of the eighteenth century in the non-functional pilasters and architrave covering steel girders and twentieth-century plumbing. The inspector had no thought to spare for the architecture. He was aware that the cheapest flats, those with three rooms only, situated under the eaves, were £5 a week, inclusive of rates. Those on the ground floor varied from £12 to £18 a week. It was a mystery to the inspector in these days when no citizen was supposed to be able to retain much more than £4,000 a year, however large his income because of income-tax and super-tax, how anyone was able to pay £18 a week for a flat in South Green. But then, he reflected, Professor Hoade was an American. Consulting the board in the hall of the left-hand block he saw that Professor Hoade was on the first floor. The hall itself was paved with some sort of composition tiles, covered in the centre with a rich blue square of Wilton carpet. There were two expensive arm-chairs, which obviously nobody had ever sat in, by the imitation fireplace, and under the window a small table supporting a vase full of imitation flowers. To the side of the entrance door was the lift, with an ornamental ironwork gate, and as there did not appear to be a staircase, the inspector entered it, and was taken up by a uniformed attendant.

'What time do you go off duty?' he asked.

'You the police?'

'Yes.'

'Round six o'clock.'

'Who relieves you?'

'They works the thing themselves in the evenings. There's a resident porter, but he's not expected to work the lift. An old lady in Number 9 always gets him out – he has a flat in the basement of the middle block – but she's not often out after six.'

'I see,' said the inspector. 'I'd like to see the porter before I go.'

Professor Hoade's flat was obviously one of those in the higher price range. The door, which was opened quietly by a discreet manservant in black coat and black bow tie, gave on to a small hall round which were several doors. It was lighted by a hanging lustre incorporating half a dozen electric candles. The man-servant ascertained his name and threw open one of the doors.

'Inspector Bruce to see you, sir.'

Professor Hoade was sitting in the window reading a copy of the *Manchester Guardian*. It was a pleasant room, not over-furnished, but what there was, was good solid stuff. There were no pictures on the walls. On the mantelpiece the inspector's keen eye observed an engraved invitation to some function of the Royal Society, and another to a soirée of the British Academy.

'Good morning,' said the Professor coming forward. 'Have you brought me a ticket?'

'A ticket for what, sir?' The inspector was momentarily put out of his stride.

'I thought I must have infringed one of your regulations with my automobile.'

'Oh, it's nothing like that, sir. I came because I heard you were an authority on manuscripts, and I wondered if you could tell me anything about Sir Arthur Dewdney.'

'Sit down, Inspector.' The Professor saw him seated in an arm-chair by the electric fire, and then sat down himself in the chair on the other side of the hearth. 'I'll tell you what I can.'

'Did you know the Bishop of Tucson, sir?'

'The Bishop of Tucson? America's a mighty big place, Inspector, and I can't say I'd ever heard of him until yesterday. I know he called at Miss Emily Dewdney's, but beyond that I can't tell you anything about him.'

'You'd heard he was dead?'

'No!' The Professor sat up abruptly and looked at the inspector with undisguised dismay. 'Dead, you say. That's just too bad. A street accident?'

'He was murdered in Miss Emily's library during the night.'

'Why, that's terrible.' The Professor had jumped to his feet, and now he walked across to the window. 'What a nasty shock for the poor old lady.'

'Oh, Miss Emily seems to be bearing up very well,' said the inspector. 'But hadn't the news reached you before now?'

'I assure you it had not, Inspector. This is the first I had heard about it.' The Professor came back from the window and flung himself into the chair he had just vacated. 'I'm an American citizen but that doesn't make me suspect number one, does it?'

'Certainly not, sir. But I thought you might be able to help me with the background. Is there or was there likely to be anything of value in Miss Emily's library, do you think? That's the first thing I want to be sure of, as it seems to supply the only possible motive. And the second thing is, was the bishop known at all in the field in which Sir Arthur Dewdney was engaged, and in which you are interested?'

'I see what you mean, Inspector.' The Professor threw one leg over the arm of the chair, and gazed for a few moments silently into the fire. The inspector said nothing.

'I am,' he began at last, 'as I think you must be aware, a great-nephew of the Jacob T. Hoade who financed Sir Arthur's last expedition, and last year I helped to write a life

90

of my great-uncle. It seems highly probable from a letter Sir Arthur wrote just before he died that he had discovered a manuscript or manuscripts of importance. You may have heard of the Chester Beatty papyri?' The inspector nodded. 'Well, it may possibly have been something of that kind, Unfortunately Sir Arthur did not live to bring his find back to England, and my great-uncle died in the same year, long before Sir Arthur's baggage arrived back in England. Frankly I came over, as my university has granted me a sabbatical year, to see if I couldn't trace the things Sir Arthur had left.'

'I take it you have had no luck as yet?'

'I only crossed over three weeks ago, and, believe it or not, I had no idea Sir Arthur had a daughter who was still alive. It gave me a kind of shock, Inspector, like living in one of those time-machine stories.'

'You were very fortunate in finding one of these flats empty.'

'I know about your housing problem.' The Professor looked quizzically at the inspector. 'But I don't think it presses quite so hard on the upper income groups. I paid around 700 dollars for the last tenant's fixtures which appeared to consist entirely of curtain runners, and that removed every difficulty.'

'I see,' said the inspector. His married sister in Twickenham had been trying all ways to get a house or even a flat of her own, but inevitably she came up across the demand for a premium, or, as it now was, a payment for so-called fixtures or junk furniture. He looked at his note-book, and then said:

'You've no idea why this bishop should suddenly come on the scene?'

'None at all, Inspector. Can I offer you a highball? I've Scotch as well as Bourbon.'

91

'No, thank you.' The inspector was not to be sidetracked. 'He wouldn't be alive when your great-uncle died, but he's never come into the picture since?'

'Not as far as I am aware.' The Professor frowned. 'You don't know what his name was?'

'Unfortunately we don't. That's the worst of bishops. So far we've got no information about him at all. We rang up Lambeth early this morning because one of the archbishop's chaplains is usually in touch with any foreign bishops who come over here – who are not Roman Catholic, of course – and he didn't know the Bishop of Tucson was in England.'

'What exactly was he doing in South Green?'

'The Vicar says he had come to see him about the possibility of his – the Vicar's – going to preach in the United States. It's just possible, of course. The bishop wouldn't know anything about the Vicar's preaching, but then why should he pick on South Green? Miss Emily's library seems to have been the real attraction. One of the first things he asked for was to be taken round there, and he was certainly found dead there.'

'It's all very odd, Inspector. If he had done any work at all in the field of palaeography, I should expect to have heard of him. Of course, he may have done it under his own name before he became a bishop.'

'We shall know more very shortly,' said the inspector. 'At the moment it looks as if he had arranged to meet someone he knew in Miss Emily's library. Possibly someone he thought had a right to be there.'

'Your difficulty is imagining a bishop breaking into someone's house. One simply cannot see a bishop of the Episcopal Church – quite the most socially conscious of our sects, Inspector – climbing down a drainpipe, or whatever he did to get out of the Vicarage unobserved, and following it up by forcing a window and climbing into the Laurels.

It just doesn't make sense.'

The snap which betrayed the broken point of the inspector's pencil revealed also a certain perturbation in the inspector's mind. He pocketed the pencil and with a ball-pointed pen wrote in his note-book:

'. . . forcing a window and climbing into the Laurels.'

For the moment, he decided against raising the matter. Instead he asked:

'This manuscript, supposing it to exist, would it be negotiable?'

'Anything coveted by a collector is negotiable, Inspector, if you know how to go about it. But with the present state of the world there would be no difficulty at all. You could say you'd bought it from someone who had smuggled it out of Russia, but you couldn't reveal his name or his family might be liquidated. Or you could have bought it from someone who was with the Partisans in Crete. There are endless possibilities. Russia is probably the best. Nobody is going to make a fuss about anything stolen from the Russians.'

'I see,' said the inspector. 'Then we might never hear of it coming on the market?'

'Almost certainly you wouldn't, Inspector. Collectors are peculiar creatures, in fact collecting is a form of mania.'

'Wouldn't a collector want others to know he'd got whatever it was?'

'A few close cronies – or rivals. But nothing would ever be heard by the general public. Some collectors are like misers, they gloat over their collections in secret, and don't care if nobody knows about them.'

'It's beyond me,' said the inspector. He got to his feet. 'I may have to come and see you again.'

'It will be a pleasure, Inspector.' The Professor also got up. 'I suppose Miss Dewdney will hardly be in a position to welcome visitors for a day or two?'

'There's no objection to visitors,' returned the inspector. 'But I'm afraid they won't be able to go into the library just yet.'

'A pity.' The Professor crossed to the door and handed over the inspector to the manservant who was hovering in the hall. 'I am still hoping to lay my hands on that manuscript of Sir Arthur's.'

CHAPTER 13

THE Vesseys' cottage, which was situated on a footpath from the East Side of the Green, parallel with Barbrook Drive but more to the south, was no longer a cottage in anything but name. Considerable sums must have been spent on it at one time or another, and the studio, built out from the north wall, proclaimed Mr. Vessey's occupation. Mr. Vessey, the inspector remembered, was not only a painter but a fashionable portrait painter, who must be earning a very considerable income from his brush. At least two members of the Royal Family had sat for him, and a Mayfair residence immediately before the Second World War had been incomplete without his interpretation of the lady of the house at the head of the staircase or over the mantelpiece in the drawing room. During the war he had preserved for posterity the features of the principal actors in the drama, and even the advent of a Labour Government had not seriously affected his income, for the wives of the new Socialist Ministers and barons were as eager to seek immortality in paint as had been the Colonels' ladies of a decade before.

The inspector glanced at the two wrought iron lamp-holders on either side of the front door, at the fresh white paint, and the untarnished chromium fittings, and then pressed the bell. Almost immediately the door was flung open by a dapper little man in a very well cut grey suit. His trim Vandyke beard alone proclaimed who he was.

'Good morning,' said the inspector. 'Could I have a few words with Mrs. Vessey.'

'No, you cannot,' said the man with the beard. 'She is not at all well.' He made as if to shut the door, a gambit to which the inspector was so accustomed that almost automatically his right toe inserted itself into the opening.

'I am sorry to be a nuisance,' he said mildly, 'but I am an officer of the Criminal Investigation Department, and I think Mrs. Vessey would probably rather see me here than receive a subpoena to appear in Court.'

'What the hell are you talking about?'

'I am enquiring into the death of an American which occurred here in South Green last night, and it seems just possible that your wife might have some information that would be of assistance to me in my investigations.'

'I have never heard such poppycock in my life.' The inspector found himself reflecting that Mr. Vessey was just the sort of person who could be expected to use such a word as poppycock. 'How could my wife have any information? I simply don't know what you're talking about.'

'Roger, honey, what is it?'

Mrs. Vessey had appeared in the hall behind her husband.

'A damned policeman saying there's been a murder, and wanting to know if you have any information about it. I've never heard such impertinence in my life. I'll ring up the Home Secretary.' Mr. Vessey became quite inarticulate with rage.

Mrs. Vessey put a hand on his arm. She was rather taller than her husband, with jet black hair and finely pointed features. At the moment she was certainly looking far from well. There were dark hollows under her eyes and her normally healthy olive complexion had a greenish tinge.

'Roger, don't be so angry. The Lieutenant has to do his duty.'

'Why, in the name of heaven, should he come to us?'

'I don't know, honey, I suppose because I'm an American. But we'd better ask him in.'

Two children passing down the footpath in the direction of the Green had paused to gaze in at the gate.

With an ill grace, the painter stood aside and allowed the inspector to enter the hall.

'Come into the studio,' said Mrs. Vessey. 'It has a good fire. We haven't been able to get a licence to put the central heating in yet, but we go on hoping.'

'I won't keep you more than a few moments,' said the inspector. He had suddenly become aware that Mrs. Vessey was very near to hysteria.

The studio was a high, bare room, the farther side from the door consisting almost entirely of glass, the bottom panes frosted. In front of the window was an enormous contraption of wood and pulleys surmounted by frames covered with white linen, apparently an apparatus to control the light. Against the right-hand wall was a dais on which was a solitary and extremely uncomfortable-looking chair, and in the middle of the floor was a large and empty easel. The floor was of parquet and beautifully polished. It was bare of rugs except in front of the fire which was in the centre of the wall opposite the dais. Two arm-chairs and a large chesterfield were grouped around it, and there were four small occasional tables, one to each arm-chair, and one at either end of the chesterfield. There were no pictures or canvases in the studio, and it looked extremely bleak except for the bright log fire in the grate.

Mrs. Vessey went across and stood on the farther side of the fireplace, with her arm running along the mantelpiece. Her fingers, the inspector noticed, kept closing and unclosing. Mr. Vessey stood glowering just inside the door.

'Do sit down, Lieutenant.'

'Inspector it is, madam.'

'I'm sorry. Inspector, then.'

'I believe you've already heard about this murder at the Laurels?'

Mrs. Vessey exchanged a glance with her husband. In the glance was certainly some element of apprehension, but the dominant emotion was something other, something which for a moment the inspector could not place. He docketed it away in his mind.

'Our servant told us when she came in this morning that some visitor staying at the Vicarage had been murdered,' said Mr. Vessey from the door. 'I fail to see what that has got to do with my wife. We just know the Vicar, but we are not church-goers, and have very little to do with him. I don't suppose we have exchanged a single word with him this year.'

'The victim,' said the inspector smoothly, 'was the Bishop of Tucson. I understand that Mrs. Vessey met him on the Green on Monday night.'

Mrs. Vessey's hand moved from the mantelpiece to her throat, but her husband broke in again before she could speak.

'My wife has been ill, Inspector. She had one of her attacks as she was coming across the Green on the night you mention. We have a car, but just at the moment we have no chauffeur, and my wife does not drive. The bus journey was too much for her. I believe she passed the Vicar and certain other people, but I fail to see' – here the note of anger came back into his voice – 'I entirely fail to see what that has got to do with the murder. It is monstrous, absolutely monstrous, that my wife should be dragged in. We know nothing whatever about this bishop. My wife had no bishop among her acquaintances in the United States, and in any case she is a Christian Scientist.'

'You had never seen him before?' asked the inspector, looking across at Mrs. Vessey.

It was at this moment that the telephone rang from somewhere out in the hall. With an irritable gesture, Mr. Vessey went out of the room to answer it.

'As my husband has said. I don't know any bishops, Inspector.'

'The call is for you, Inspector,' said Mr. Vessey reappearing at the door.

'Thank you, sir,' said the inspector. 'I am sorry to have given you this trouble and to have upset Mrs. Vessey. But a murder is a murder.'

'The sooner you get on the murderer's track the better,' said Mr. Vessey acidly. His temper was rather more under control, but he was still quivering a little with rage. The artistic temperament, thought the inspector.

He followed Mr. Vessey into the hall, and was shown a white ivory instrument standing on a small black oak table.

'Inspector Bruce here.'

'Oh, is that you, Mr. Bruce. The Super wants you. Here you are, sir.'

'Hallo, sir. Bruce here.'

'Bruce, a most extraordinary thing has happened. You'd better drop what you're doing and come round straight away.'

'Yes, sir?'

'We've just had a cable passed on to us from the Assistant Commissioner. It's from the Bishop of Tucson, in Paris.'

'What?'

'It says: "Report of my death much exaggerated. Staying American Club, Boulevard Raspail, Paris until end of week. Bishop of Tucson." What do you think of that?'

'Then who is this chap at the Vicarage?'

'That's just what you're going to have to find out. I think you'd better come back here before you interview anyone else, and we'll ring up this bishop at the club in Paris. It may be a hoax, of course.'

'I'll be round in five minutes,' said the inspector, and hung up.

Mr. Vessey was standing by the front door, his hand on the knob, ready to let him out.

'Just a moment,' said the inspector. 'I've left my hat.' He stepped through the studio door to retrieve his hat from the chesterfield, and surprised Mrs. Vessey, slumped in the armchair on the farther side of the fireplace, her head buried in her arms, sobbing as if her heart would break.

The inspector said nothing. Apparently she did not even notice him. He took up his hat and went out again.

'I'm afraid I shall have to look in again sometime later,' he said.

Mr. Vessey did not reply, but silently opened the door.

'Good morning,' said the inspector.

There was still no reply. The door closed silently behind him.

'There's something very wrong there,' said the inspector to himself, as he turned away from the Green and made for the police station. 'She's scared stiff about something. And an innocent citizen wouldn't put on an act like his. Ring up the Home Secretary my foot! Of course, she's an American, and he may feel protective, but I should have thought Americans were well able to take care of themselves these days.' The inspector shook his head. 'She never said whether she recognized the bishop. Damn it,' he added. 'She said "I don't know any bishops", and now it appears he isn't a bishop at all. I'd wager anything she knows who he is, but whether or not she's implicated in the murder or not is another matter.' He stopped and extracted the note-book from his pocket. In front of Mrs. Vessey in the list of suspects he wrote 'Mr. &'. 'If he got really mad,' said the inspector to himself, 'I wouldn't put it past him to crown anyone with a pair of fire-tongs, or anything else that happened to be handy.'

CHAPTER 14

'THIS is a nice how-do-you-do and no mistake,' said the Superintendent cheerfully as Inspector Bruce entered his office. Superintendent Frazer was a well set-up, military-looking man, just beginning to run to fat. He was within two years of his retirement. It was at South Green that he had reached the rank of Inspector in the uniformed branch, and had then been transferred to another district, only returning as Superintendent on the death of Miss Hogg's father. He and Superintendent Hogg had been friends since they had pounded a beat together, and they had always remained on the most cordial terms. 'I've put in a personal call to the Bishop of Tucson at the American Club, so we shall see what we shall see. Or hear rather,' he corrected himself. 'You always did say there was something fishy about this bishop at Miss Emily's.'

'I wonder how the real bishop got to hear about the murder so quickly,' said the inspector.

'You must ask him. How is our friend Flora getting on, by the way?'

'As fit as a fiddle and full of beans,' replied the inspector. 'As a matter of fact she's given me a good deal of useful information about Sir Arthur, though at the moment it's rather difficult to see how it all fits in.'

'I wonder what the old Super would have said if he could have seen his little Flora launching out like this. I remember him arguing once that the greatest disservice Hitler did to civilization was when he maintained that woman's place was the home. Not because he was wrong but because he was right. He said the bad things Hitler did discredited the good ones, and they were all dragged down together. He's told me many a time that the increase in juvenile delinquency dates from the day women got the vote.'

'I don't think it's entirely true.'

'There's some truth in it. A lot of these dead-end kids who end up in Borstal would never have got into the courts if the mother hadn't been working in a factory or a shop instead of looking after the home. But I'll grant you housing has a lot to do with it. And the cost of living which forces the women into the factories.'

'Which is due to the war,' put in the inspector.

'And getting ready for the next one. It all adds up. But what people don't see,' went on the Superintendent, taking out a packet of cigarette papers and beginning to roll a cigarette from a pouch on the desk in front of him, 'what they don't see is that if there hadn't been this emancipation of women, wages for men would have been relatively higher today, so that they could support a wife and family.'

'Actually,' said the inspector argumentatively, 'there was more juvenile crime in early Victorian days than there is now. And it was due to poverty.'

'And gin,' the Superintendent said.

A buzzer sounded on his desk.

'That's your call,' he said. 'You take it.'

'Hullo,' said the inspector into the instrument.

'Your call to Paris, sir,' said the constable on the switchboard. 'The Bishop of Tucson.'

'Is this London?' asked an American voice. 'The Bishop of Tucson here. I understand I've just been murdered over in your city.'

'Inspector Bruce speaking, from the South Green Police Station.'

'Pleased to know you, Inspector. Can you tell me what this is all about?'

'I'm sorry to say there has been a murder, and until we had your cable we understood it was the Bishop of Tucson. Is there any possibility of your being able to come over to London for twenty-four hours?'

'Well, I'm on vacation. I guess I could take a plane over if you think it really necessary.'

'There's a possibility you may be able to identify the body. I could bring photographs over to you if that would be more convenient for you, but I really think it would be much better if you could come over yourself.'

'If I can get a reservation, I'll be over on the afternoon plane.'

'That's very good of you. We'll see you get a reservation, and I'll meet you at Northolt. Before you ring off, sir, how did you come to hear about the murder?'

'It was on the tape here in the club at breakfast-time. I was having breakfast, rather late I'm afraid, and one of the club boys came over and told me.'

'I see.' The inspector scratched his head with his free hand, and looked across at the Superintendent, who shook his head. 'I think that's all at the moment, sir. I'll get B.E.A. to reserve you a seat – you can ring the Paris office and confirm the time in about half an hour from now – and I'll meet you at the airport. It's very good of you to help us.'

'Not at all, Inspector. I don't like hearing I've been murdered. Gave me quite a shock. I'm wanting to get to the bottom of it myself.'

'You've got this chap's finger-prints at Miss Emily's?' enquired the Superintendent, as the inspector replaced the receiver. The Superintendent, who had acquired a respect for rank coincident with his own rise in the police hierarchy, would never have referred thus even to a dead bishop. It made it clear that he had accepted him as an imposter.

'Yes, sir. I suppose we'd better send them over to the F.B.I. by the next plane. As soon as I've arranged the bishop's reservation for this afternoon.'

'It looks to me as if you won't be able to get very far until you know who exactly he is. He might be this Professor Hoade's cousin, or Mrs. Vessey's brother. On the other hand, he may be just a chance burglar who'd heard exaggerated stories of Miss Emily's treasures.'

'Hardly a chance burglar, sir. The impersonation is surely too elaborate for that.'

'I only meant he may not be connected with anybody in South Green at all.'

'Except that someone in South Green certainly murdered him.'

'Before you go,' said the Superintendent, 'did you get anything out of the people you called on this morning?'

'Nothing of any real importance. But in every case there was an undercurrent of something I don't like.'

The Superintendent snorted, in order to express his opinion of undercurrents.

'You put two and two together, my lad,' he said, 'and sooner or later you'll get somewhere. But for God's sake don't let's have too much psychology. You can leave that to our Flora. I know it's all the rage these days, but it never got a policeman anywhere. You try feeding psychology to the Judge of Assize and see where it gets you.'

'I should like to know where Sir Wellington Orde was in the small hours of this morning,' said the inspector. 'Lady Orde was scared stiff. But you can't ask her straight out whether he was in bed with her at the material time. And they may be one of these modern couples who sleep in separate beds.'

'What was the material time?' asked the Superintendent.

'Just on one o'clock,' replied the inspector. 'Perhaps ten minutes before.'

'If you think the Ordes had anything whatever to do with it, you'll have to get their alibis, of course. But I'd wait until you know for certain who the chap is.'

The inspector excused himself, and went out to make arrangements for securing the Bishop of Tucson's reservation, which had to be done through the proper channels, and sending the bogus bishop's finger-prints to the Federal Bureau of Investigation, Washington, D.C.

He dropped in again to see the Superintendent before going round to the Laurels.

'That man Vessey,' he said, 'threatened to ring the Home Secretary this morning.'

'Let him,' said the Superintendent. 'What's his trouble?'

'Miss Hogg was coming out of the Laurels on Monday night when she ran into the Vicar and this chap who was murdered. They were apparently just strolling round the Green. After she met them and while they were still talking, Mrs. Vessey came along North Side from the bus stop. Just before she got up to them, she fainted. Miss Hogg is quite clear that the reason she fainted was because she caught sight of this bishop.'

'Bogus bishop,' put in the Superintendent.

'Sir. I'm only referring to him as the bishop until I find something else to call him. But it seems clear Mrs. Vessey recognized him.'

'Wouldn't she tell you anything?'

'She made a quite obvious prevarication. But they were both of them far more worked up about the murder this morning than they had any right to be if they were innocent. I don't mean,' he hastened to add, 'that I think Mrs. Vessey did it, though I can't strike either her or her husband off the list of possible suspects. But they know something, and in some way it appears to be discreditable to Mrs. Vessey. At least that's how I read it.'

'I suppose she could have done it, physically speaking?'

'Oh, anyone could have knocked the chap out with that pair of fire-tongs. And apparently he was kneeling by one of Sir Arthur's boxes. Which looks as if he knew the person, more or less. If it had been a stranger, he would surely have got to his feet.'

'What I don't seem to fathom is why this bogus bishop should go to all this trouble to meet someone in a completely strange house after midnight in South Green. Did he have a phone call after he got to the Vicarage?'

'No, according to the Vicar they just sat round the fire after supper, and went to bed soon after ten o'clock. The Vicar had earlier on asked Mrs. Vessey to make a fourth at bridge, but naturally after the episode on the Green she cancelled it, saying she didn't feel well. Which reminds me, Vessey was far too quick in denying that they had anything to do with the Vicar. If I remember rightly he said that they hadn't exchanged a single word with him this year, which must be untrue if Mrs. Vessey had arranged to go in there to bridge.'

'She may be very keen on bridge,' said the Superintendent. 'People who are really keen will play with persons they wouldn't dream of acknowledging socially, if it's a question of making up a four.'

'It shows how scared they were, though. They hadn't had time to think up a proper story, so Vessey resorted to blind denials of every connection with the bishop and the Vicarage.'

'The Vicar never noticed anything wrong about this bogus bishop?'

'Nothing very much. He put any oddness down to his being an American.'

'Naturally,' said the Superintendent. 'But he must have had it all planned out.' He reached for his pouch and began

106

to roll another cigarette. 'You know if some American policeman came to stay with me, I'm pretty sure I should rumble him if he weren't a policeman at all, considerable as the difference is between our ideas and theirs.'

'I think the Vicar was probably day-dreaming most of the time about this preaching engagement in the States.'

'I heard the Vicar on Armistice Sunday last year. I wouldn't say he'd set the Thames on fire, or the Hudson, I suppose I should say. But I don't suppose Vicars know in the least what their own sermons are like. They never have to sit and listen to them. Well, my lad, use soft soap with these nobs of yours on the Green, and put two and two together, and then four and four, and you'll get somewhere in the end. I must get on with this rape case for the Sessions tomorrow. He says it's all a mistake due to his American trousers. There seems to be American influence at work wherever you turn.'

'American trousers?' The inspector sounded startled.

The Superintendent gave a deep, rumbling chuckle. 'They have a zip instead of buttons. He says something had gone wrong with the zip, and the woman mistook his intentions.'

CHAPTER 15

A⊤ about the same time as the inspector was closeted with the Superintendent, Miss Hogg and her friend Milly were calling at the Laurels. The house appeared to be in a state of siege. This, they soon discovered, was because of the newspaper reporters who had been swarming round the premises from an early hour. Phyllis Maud had the front door on the chain, but when she realized who it was she quickly let them in, and then bolted the door again behind them.

'Dreadful young men,' she said, 'with no respect for anybody or anything. One of them took a photo of me,' she added rather complacently.

'You'll be in the evening papers,' said Miss Hogg.

'Do you think so, miss.' Plainly Phyllis Maud was not at all alarmed at the prospect. 'I hope Miss Emily won't mind.'

'Not she,' said Miss Hogg.

'I should have thought anything like this here would have been the death of her,' said Phyllis Maud. 'But she's as right as a ninepin this morning.'

'The Victorians were a good deal tougher than we are,' said Miss Hogg.

'It's all these anaesthetics and things,' put in Milly.

The police had gone, but had left the library locked up. Miss Emily, who received them in the drawing-room upstairs where a cheerful fire was burning, told them that it would most probably be opened up again in the afternoon when the inspector had had one more look round.

'A very nice policeman with the reddest hair has advised me to have screws put in the downstairs window-frames,' she said. 'He showed me how easy it is to push the catches back with a penknife. I told him I'd lived in the house for

108

eighty-three years and it hardly seemed worth while making alterations at this late hour.'

'Like bolting the stable door when the horse has been stolen,' agreed Milly.

'I don't know,' said Miss Hogg. 'We're hoping that Sir Arthur discovered something really valuable, and if they haven't got it already, we're going to find it ourselves.'

'We should all be famous!' exclaimed Milly, and blushed when they both looked at her.

'I'm afraid, my dear, fame means very little to an old woman of eighty-three. But I should like to think Sir Arthur had a little honour paid him. He would appreciate it, wherever he happens to be.' She spoke as if Sir Arthur were on one of his expeditions, perhaps a little farther than Transcaucasia.

'They haven't stopped at murder,' Miss Hogg reminded her soberly. 'And if they haven't got what they were after, they are almost sure to try again as soon as the hue and cry has died down.'

'You may be right,' said Miss Emily. 'And it wouldn't be fair on Phyllis Maud. And that reminds me that one of Sir Arthur's boxes is in my bedroom. The reason is it was his tuck box at school, and he always used to take it with him when he went abroad. When it came back with all the other things my mother put it in her bedroom for sentimental reasons, and now it's in mine.'

'Why, that may have in it the very thing we're looking for,' said Miss Hogg excitedly.

'I'm afraid not, my dear. It's really full of the most dreadful rubbish. I don't suppose Sir Arthur packed anything; his bearers would just put his things into the boxes as they came to hand. He was very like a jackdaw. Or do I mean a magpie? There's a bag of rather odd pebbles with a note by Sir Arthur that the peasants used to carry one sewn into their clothes as a cure for rheumatism. And there are some old books, and various manuscript pages like the ones downstairs, but I'm afraid they're not at all valuable.'

'The bearers must have been very honest,' said Milly.

'I think they were rather frightened of Sir Arthur,' said Miss Emily with a smile. 'I remember my mother telling me they thought he was quite a magician. He had a wonderful beard and moustache.'

'May we look at this box?' asked Miss Hogg.

'Certainly, my dear. But you'll have to come into my bedroom because the box is rather too heavy to carry in here. I'll ask Phyllis Maud to bring up the cake and Madeira wine, and then we'll go and have a look.'

Miss Emily's bedroom across the landing was a perfect mid-Victorian period piece, from the enormous mahogany wardrobe with two mirror-framed doors to the vast bed which, though not a four-poster, had a canopy at its head from which descended red curtains fringed with pompoms. The bed level was more than four feet from the floor, and Miss Hogg was fascinated to see a small step-ladder with three steps at the side of the bed.

Sir Arthur's tuck box turned out to be a splendid affair in what Miss Hogg took to be rosewood. It stood beside the dressing-table in a window which looked over the garden. There were now no direct traces of its journeys on its outer surface, for it had obviously been the recipient of a loving expenditure of beeswax, turpentine and elbow-grease in the course of the last half-century and more. But inside, the contents were very much like those of the boxes downstairs. Miss Hogg squatted on her heels in front of it, and lifted out the top tray.

'We might lift it on to the bed,' suggested Miss Emily.

'Oh, no, it's quite all right,' said Miss Hogg. She tried to keep the disappointment out of her voice. As Miss Emily had remarked, Sir Arthur seemed to have emulated the jackdaw and the magpie. He really had accumulated the most awful lot of rubbish. She lifted out a yellowish canvas bag which was remarkably heavy for its size and shook part of its contents on to the floor.

'That's the rheumatism cure,' said Miss Emily. 'Oddly enough I've never suffered from rheumatism, so I've never needed to try it. Sir Arthur used to have gout. It was more fashionable in those days.'

The pebbles, as Miss Emily had called them, appeared to be lumps of granite inlaid with veins and nodules of some black substance. Rather like flint in chalk, Miss Hogg remarked to herself. Or fossilized cobbler's wax. She had come into contact with cobbler's wax in her early days at the County Girls' School, for one of the girls had left a flattened lump on her chair, with disastrous results to the almost new tweed skirt she had been wearing.

'I might take them up to someone at the Science Museum,' she said doubtfully. 'You never know. I don't think it can possibly be gold, but it might be something valuable for all that.'

'Shale,' suggested Milly. 'I don't really know what it looks like, but isn't it what they get oil from?'

'It might be shale,' agreed Miss Hogg. 'Though I've no idea what shale looks like either. If you don't mind,' she added, turning to Miss Emily, 'I'll take these up to the Science Museum tomorrow or Friday. I'm going up to the Burghley Library this afternoon.'

'Do as you please,' said Miss Emily. 'That tin which says Monkey Brand actually has some manuscript pages inside it, but they don't look to be of any particular value.'

Miss Hogg shook the roll of parchment on to the floor. It resolved itself into four yellowed pages, covered with faded, rust-coloured writing in letters which were, Miss Hogg recognized, Greek capitals.

'They'd do beautifully to make a lampshade,' she said.

'You can have them, my dear,' said Miss Emily. 'They might just as well be doing something useful. They'll all be thrown away, most probably, when I'm dead.'

'I should love them,' said Miss Hogg absently, rolling them up again, and putting them back in the tin. She got to her feet, after replacing the tray and closing the tuck box. 'I'll get an expert opinion about these stones, but I must say they feel rather like lead.'

'Come and have a glass of Madeira wine,' said Miss Emily, leading the way back to the drawing-room. 'It is rather dreadful to think that only this time yesterday I was giving that American bishop a glass out of the same decanter.'

It was as they were about to leave some half an hour later that Miss Emily suggested they should first take a look at her Easter lilies which were in full bloom in the garden. Miss Emily slipped on what she called her gardening coat, and they went out through the door at the end of the passage by the library. On the path as they came out was a large smoky Persian cat playing with what looked like a metal tube that shone as it caught the sunlight.

'This is Sarah,' observed Miss Emily. 'I don't think you've met her before.'

Sarah took no notice of them, but rolled over on her back on the gravel path, and tossed the object she was playing with up into the air.

With an exclamation, Miss Hogg darted forward and retrieved the thing, which proved to be a gold propelling pencil. With an injured air, Sarah got up and stalked away, her tail high, and twitching at the tip.

Miss Hogg turned the pencil round. Engraved on it were the initials 'W. O.'

'I must show this to the inspector,' she said.

'Is it a clue?' asked Milly breathlessly.

'It may be. Has Sir Wellington ever looked round your garden?' she asked Miss Emily.

'Not to my knowledge,' replied Miss Emily. 'He's only been to see me twice, you know, and it was the library he was interested in.'

They walked across the lawn and admired the lilies. Miss Hogg hardly saw them, for she took off her pince-nez as they stood by the bed and polished them vigorously. Milly, however, who was knowledgeable about flowers, went into raptures, and said enough for both of them.

They were turning away when a man in a check suit suddenly climbed on to the wall that separated Miss Emily's garden from that of Mr. Bartley Craig and levelled a large camera at them.

'What a rude young puppy,' said Miss Emily in a voice that certainly carried as far as the young man in question. 'Phyllis Maud loves being photographed, of course. Such a tragedy, I think, that newspapers seem to be run almost entirely by the servant class today.'

CHAPTER 16

Big Ben was pointing to twenty minutes past two as Miss Hogg came up out of the underground at Westminster on the Wednesday afternoon. She crossed by the policeman at the top of Whitehall, walked round the north and west sides of Parliament Square, waited for a suitable opportunity to cross Victoria Street, and then proceeded down Great Smith Street until she came to the opening which led to St. Stephen's Square. As the Burghley Library had no number, at least none was given in *Whitaker*, she kept right round the Square right-handed until she was almost back at her starting point, when it became apparent that the grey stone building on the left of the passage by which she had entered the Square was the Burghley Library. Sitting in a glass box at the end of a counter which displayed a number of rather fly-blown postcards was a withered-looking ancient in a blue uniform ornamented with black piping.

'Is this the Burghley Library?' asked Miss Hogg, just to make sure it hadn't been taken over by the Income Tax people or one of those expanding Ministries which are gradually eating up the London squares.

'It is,' croaked the ancient. 'There's no charge.'

'Could I see Dr. Greenwood?'

'Have you an appointment?'

'I haven't, but I'm an old friend of his. At least,' said Miss Hogg candidly, 'I was at college with him.'

This put the ancient rather out of his depth as, to his knowledge, no college friend had called on the librarian before, but he bent to a peculiar kind of box on the bench in front of him, clamped on a pair of headphones, and vigorously turned a somewhat wheezy handle. There was a crackle and a metallic squeaking, and then he spoke into a mouthpiece in the front of the box.

'Is the doctor up there?'

A sustained crackling and squeaking came from the earphones.

'What name, miss?' asked the old man.

'Miss Hogg, say, of Bristol University.'

This information was bellowed into the mouthpiece, and there was a further round of crackling. The porter took off the earphones, and said resignedly:

'Mr. Wimbush is coming down. He'll see to you.'

Mr. Wimbush proved to be a dapper little man with sandy hair and horn-rimmed glasses through which he peered somewhat deprecatingly at the world. He came down the broad stone staircase from the floor above at a brisk pace, and said as he came towards Miss Hogg:

'I suppose it's the Harland Bequest you wish to see?'

'I've never heard of the Harland Bequest,' replied Miss Hogg. 'I actually wanted to see Dr. Greenwood.'

'Never heard of the Harland Bequest!' exclaimed Mr. Wimbush. 'Dear me, can there really be a person who has never heard of it?' He peered at Miss Hogg as if she were indeed a rare specimen. 'It's probably the finest collection of *Erotica* in the world – outside the Vatican library, of course. They have everything. I'm so sorry. Whenever anyone asks for the librarian it's almost always because they want to see the Harland Bequest and don't like to say so to the porter.'

'Oh!' said Miss Hogg. There didn't seem much else she could say.

'It's odd how they don't mind asking Dr. Greenwood, but they don't like letting the porter know what they're after.'

'I can assure you I really do want to see the librarian. It's a personal matter. We were at Bristol together.'

'Come along up, then,' said Mr. Wimbush. 'He's not doing anything at the moment. I'm so sorry about the Harland collection. I can see it wouldn't be your line of country at all.' Miss Hogg gave him a scowl as she took in the import of this, to which Mr. Wimbush appeared completely oblivious. 'You'd be surprised how many people do come here just to see it. It's about the only thing they do come here to see,' he added gloomily.

They had gone up the stone flight of stairs, and down a long corridor lined on either side with leather-backed folios in eighteenth-century shelves, and passed through a door marked 'Private' into a room where an elderly lady sat at a small desk manipulating a typewriter. Opposite the door by which they had entered was another door with a panel of frosted glass on which was stencilled the word 'Librarian'. Mr. Wimbush knocked on this door, opened it, and stood aside for Miss Hogg to enter.

'A visitor to see you, sir,' he said.

Dr. Greenwood had aged considerably in the twenty years since Miss Hogg had last seen him propping up the wall while gloomily watching Emmie Pargeter performing the fox-trot or the valeta on the Bristol dance-floor. He was almost completely bald, and his skin had the bleached appearance of one who rarely sees the daylight.

'Good afternoon,' he said. He was sitting behind a large desk on which was an inkstand, a blotting-pad, In and Out trays, both empty, and a telephone, of the type which has an earphone hooked on at the side, and he made no effort to get up. In front of him was a small volume which he closed quickly as they came into the room. It was probably, Miss Hogg reflected, an item from the Harland Bequest. He indicated a chair. Mr. Wimbush withdrew, closing the door quietly behind him.

'What can I do for you?' he asked.

'I don't expect you remember me. My name's Hogg. I was a friend of Emmie Pargeter's at Bristol.'

'Indeed,' said Dr. Greenwood. 'Emmie Judson she is now. You don't take the *Old Students' Chronicle*?'

'I do, but I must have missed Emmie's getting married.'

'She was very fond of dancing,' said Dr. Greenwood, 'but now, I understand, she has five children, so I don't suppose she indulges in it quite so much as she used to.'

'She never did believe in half-measures,' said Miss Hogg.

'But,' said Dr. Greenwood briskly, 'you obviously didn't come here to discuss Emmie Judson. Is it some book or manuscript you want to see?'

'It's about manuscripts. I don't know if you remember Milly Brown, who was also up the same time we were. Well, she's staying with me at the moment, and we remembered you, and I decided to come and ask your help. Do you know the name of Sir Arthur Dewdney?'

'Well, yes, I do. In a vague sort of way. But he's been dead a long time, surely?'

'Eighty years, to be exact. But he left a number of boxes full of things he'd acquired on his last expedition.' She plunged into a brief description of what had been happening at the Laurels in the last few days. 'What we want is expert help to go over the manuscripts. And if there were a real find, you could have the honour and glory of finding it,' she concluded magnanimously.

'Thank you,' said Dr. Greenwood. 'But it might be rather a tall order. On the other hand it might be quite exciting.' He grinned engagingly, and for a moment the twenty years fell away, and he was the young man who had bicycled out into Somerset and Gloucester to rub obscure brasses and copy the crumbling inscriptions of forgotten memorials. 'What I can't understand is why no one has ever gone through the things before this. There must have been quite

117

a number of people interested at the time.'

'The American who was the chief interested party died very soon after Sir Arthur, and before the boxes got back to England. And then the relatives in America never bothered about them.'

'I suppose this American bishop wasn't some relative of Sir Arthur's patron?'

'I don't think so, or Professor Hoade would surely have known about him.'

'Professor Hoade. Do you mean Amos T. Hoade?'

'Yes. Do you know him?'

'I know of him, of course. And that reminds me we've got a book by him or one of his relations. It came in only the other day.' He pressed a bell at the side of the desk, and the elderly lady from the ante-room put her head round the door. 'Oh, Miss Brett, have you the book that came in the other day by an American called Hoade? It was going into Biographies, I think, though there was some question about a cross-classification.'

Miss Brett made no reply, but simply withdrew. They waited in silence. In a very short space of time she was back with a large square volume in a cream dust cover.

'This is the volume, doctor,' she said, and laid it reverently on his desk. Then she gave him a swift, coy look, and retreated backwards, as though withdrawing from the presence of royalty. 'She's sweet on him,' thought Miss Hogg.

'Here we are,' said Dr. Greenwood. He took up the book and turned to the title-page, and then glanced at the short list of acknowledgements which included the name of Prof. Amos T. Hoade 'for much valuable help, and for the letters on pp. 89, 91 and 107'. Finally he turned to the index, and then flipped back a few pages.

'Here is the last letter Sir Arthur Dewdney ever wrote,' he said. Miss Hogg bent over the desk and read it with him.

It was given in facsimile on the page facing the letterpress, but the print was easier to read. From a glance at the illustration, Miss Hogg saw that Sir Arthur had used the long *s*.

Jacob T. Hoade, Esqre.,
MY DEAR SIR,

I am sorry to have to inform you that I am laid low with a fever, but I have found something which will be of great interest to you, even if it be not all that you require. Tomorrow I hope to be well enough to complete the negotiations with the monks. They are Monophysites, which accounts for their having travelled so far; and they long for new books and new heresies, for which they are more than willing to exchange the old. If I do not take a turn for the worse, I shall be carried down to Tiflis sometime next week, and I should reach Trebizond next month.

Believe me to be, dear Sir,
Your obdt. servant,
ARTHUR DEWDNEY.

'It's very vague,' said Dr. Greenwood. 'I suppose,' he added, 'the monks had gone there to get away from the Nestorians.'

'No mention of a gold-mine,' said Miss Hogg in disappointed tones.

'I know very little about the science of geology,' replied Dr. Greenwood. 'But I do not think there are any important gold deposits in Transcaucasia. There may be anything there, of course, almost literally anything, but as the area is now well behind the Iron Curtain it is of little interest to anyone in the West.'

'It might be interesting from a strategic point of view,' urged Miss Hogg, fighting a rearguard action for her gold-mine.

'What he certainly seems to have discovered is a manuscript of some kind. But we are entirely in the dark as to whether he did eventually secure it, and whether it was in his effects when they were sent back to England. From such knowledge as I have of things ecclesiastical, I should think it highly probable that the monks would have recovered their manuscript on the death of Sir Arthur, and retained their *quid pro quo* at the same time.'

'Monophysites, or whatever you call them, may have a higher sense of morality than ordinary monks.'

'More than doubtful. Monks have no morals, whether orthodox or heretical.' It was evident that Dr. Greenwood was a confirmed Protestant. His pronouncements had all the assurance of an *ex cathedra* infallibility. 'Your only hope is that the manuscript in question was one of which they did not realize the value. In that case it may still be in Sir Arthur's boxes.'

'And that's what we want you to come over and find out for us.'

Dr. Greenwood pursed his lips.

'I am rather fully occupied at the moment,' he said. 'But I will look in my little book.' He took out a small pocket diary, and turned over a few pages. As far as Miss Hogg could see, they were almost entirely blank. 'I could come over the day after tomorrow, rather late in the afternoon.'

'That's very kind of you,' said Miss Hogg gratefully. 'You'd better come to my house first, and I'll take you round to Miss Emily's.' She gave him concise directions as to his route, and got up to go.

'I'm quite sure we're going to find something wonderful,' she said.

Miss Brett frowned as she passed her.

'You silly thing,' Miss Hogg thought to herself. 'You can have him. Our relationship is purely business.'

CHAPTER 17

Miss Hogg, back from the Burghley Library, and her friend, Milly Brown, were just about to sit down to high tea at half past six when Inspector Bruce called round at the house in Acacia Avenue. He had just sent the Bishop of Tucson, the real bishop this time, of that there was no doubt, in a police car up to the Savoy, where the bishop had arranged to stay the night.

All this was news to Miss Hogg, who had not yet heard that the original bishop was an imposter.

'I don't quite see what it all means at the moment,' she said, polishing her pince-nez vigorously and absent-mindedly on the oven cloth, which Milly had draped over the back of a chair. 'It doesn't alter the fact that they were after something or other Sir Arthur had discovered all those years ago.'

She had taken the inspector into the cosy little living-room at the back of the house, where a modern grate combined an oven with an open fireplace.

'Have you had a meal today?' she asked, coming back abruptly to the present, and fixing the inspector with a schoolmarm eye. 'You look about all in.'

'I had some sandwiches at the airport while I was waiting,' said the inspector.

'Sandwiches at the airport,' snorted Miss Hogg. 'Are they any better than railway sandwiches? You must just sit down and have some of Milly's chicken. She brought it up from Essex with her, and she's even cooked it while I've been traipsing about in town. But I've got an expert to come and look through Sir Arthur's boxes, by the way.'

The inspector needed little persuading. Milly was on the point of taking the chicken out of the oven, and having put it on a dish, she went into the kitchen proper to fetch the potatoes from the gas stove, followed by a dish of green peas on which she had extravagantly put a lump of butter.

'They're fresh peas from the Scilly Islands,' Miss Hogg informed the inspector. 'Or the Canaries. I can't remember which. Hideously expensive, but very nice for once. Milly! I can smell something burning.'

'Oh, dear,' exclaimed Milly, 'it's the bread sauce.' And she dashed back into the kitchen.

'Just tip it out, and don't scrape it off the bottom of the pan,' Miss Hogg called after her. She was carving dexterously, having always done it in the Superintendent's time.

'In the ordinary way,' said the inspector, reverting to the main topic under discussion, 'we should have asked Sir Wellington Orde to run through the manuscripts, but somehow he seems to be involved.'

'Oh, my goodness!' exclaimed Miss Hogg in dismay. 'I've been withholding essential evidence.' She rushed out into the hall for her bag, and came back to hand the gold pencil she had found that morning to the inspector. 'I'm terribly sorry I forgot about it. I slipped it into my bag because I didn't want Miss Emily to start asking questions, and then with that idiotic reporter taking our photographs I forgot all about it.'

'It gives me something else to question him on,' said the inspector. 'Where exactly was it?'

'On the path outside the door that leads to the library from the garden. The cat was playing with it, and she may have rolled it from the bed under the library window, but it isn't the sort of thing she could move very far.'

'He may have lost it in the ordinary course of events,' said the inspector, slipping the pencil into his pocket.

'Except that Miss Emily is quite definite he never went into the garden on the two occasions he has been to the house.'

122

'What I haven't told you yet,' said the inspector, 'is this bogus bishop's real name. The first thing I did when I met the real bishop was to run him round to the mortuary, and he recognized the man immediately. Didn't remember his name, but he'd been on the boat with him coming over. The real bishop had even had a game of bridge with him. I'd already found what boat it was they'd come to Europe on, so I had a passenger list. We ran through the names, and he remembered it as soon as he saw it. Milligan.'

'So now we can refer to him in future by his proper name, thank goodness,' said Miss Hogg.

'Instead of as a wolf in sheep's clothing,' put in Milly.

'If it is his proper name,' said the inspector gloomily. 'Still, it'll do to go on with.'

'Now whatever do you mean?' asked Miss Hogg, helping herself to some more peas.

'Milligan may be just the name he assumed to come to Europe. He must have decided to change identities with the bishop when he found the bishop was getting off at Cherbourg, and not coming to England. It was fairly safe for a day or two. The outfit was easy enough to get, especially as American bishops don't wear gaiters and all that paraphernalia. Anybody can buy a clerical collar. What we're trying to find now is his luggage that came from America with him. Obviously the stuff at the Vicarage had been bought for the occasion. He lunched at the Grandiose on the Sunday, and it was then he wrote to the Vicar, and he lunched there again on the Monday and was picked up there by the car hire people. But we haven't been able to find where he spent Saturday and Sunday nights. We're showing his photograph to all the taxi-men in London, so we may find one who dropped him at the Grandiose. If he took a taxi.'

'Cheer up,' said Miss Hogg. 'Think how awful it is for me. My first case, and there's almost nothing I can do. In fact I think detective work is going to be much more difficult than I had imagined. It's all right in books, with the body found in a library and all that.' She took off her pince-nez and blinked at the inspector as she polished them on her table napkin. 'Of course you'll tell me the body *was* found in a library. But in the classic sense, it wasn't. It might just as well have been a railway station.'

'How?' asked Milly, who had paused in her dissection of a wing to listen to her friend. 'I just don't follow you, Hogg.'

'The body in the library gag,' explained Miss Hogg, 'has your detective and all the suspects staying in some country house with the victim. And if he's lucky, there's deep snow all round, with six-foot drifts on the roads. And then the detective has an easy time because he can question all his fellow-guests quite naturally. Can you see me getting an opportunity to question Sir Wellington Orde?'

'It's difficult, I can see that,' agreed Milly. 'But I'm sure you'll think of something, Hogg.'

'We shall know more about Milligan tomorrow, any-way,' put in the inspector. 'His prints are even now crossing the Atlantic. Reminds you of Crippen.'

'Crippen?' enquired Milly.

'He was the first man caught by telegraph across the Atlantic,' explained Miss Hogg kindly. She was well up in her criminology.

'The name Crippen always gives me the shudders,' said Milly.

'It's so stupid using his name as a sort of bogy,' said Miss Hogg. 'All he did was to give his wife an overdose of hyoscine hydrobromide by mistake, to keep her quiet while he entertained Miss Le Neve. It's the stuff you take every time you cross the Channel,' she added, with the air of a veteran globe-trotter. Mr. Dalrymple had introduced her to the little tablets on the Dover to Calais run, though she had not needed them on the journey back.

The inspector pushed back his plate.

'That was fine,' he said. 'I know it isn't done in the best of circles, but I shall just have to leave you.'

'Oh,' wailed Milly, 'you must just try my trifle. I'm afraid I couldn't get the mock cream to go quite stiff enough, but I'm sure it tastes all right.'

The inspector repressed a shudder, as Milly brought in a large glass bowl full of what appeared to be custard, covered with a whitish substance on which had been liberally sprinkled hundreds and thousands, definitely the nastier kind made of some sort of edible plastic.

'I'm not a great one for sweets,' he said pleadingly, but Milly was already spooning out a lavish helping. 'Steady now, I've got to go and call on Mrs. Vessey again.'

'I don't really know her,' put in Miss Hogg. 'In fact yesterday was the first time I ever spoke to her, I think. But she didn't seem a murderer to me.'

'I don't say she is,' said the inspector, manfully tackling his trifle. 'Though you'd be surprised what sort of people can take to murder when they're pushed. But from what you told me, and from her attitude this morning, I should say she knows something about this man Milligan.'

'Yes,' said Miss Hogg reflectively. 'I'm sure it was seeing the bishop – Milligan, that is – that bowled her over. It couldn't have been me, or the Vicar, and she can't have a phobia about clergymen, because the Vicar said something about her going round to play bridge there. She just caught sight of Milligan, and down she went.'

'Milligan himself never gave any sign of recognition, I suppose?'

'I wasn't paying much attention to him at the time. Naturally the Vicar and I went to help Mrs. Vessey. But he didn't seem to recognize her. He just stood there, and in a way that's rather odd in itself. I mean you'd expect him to try and lend a hand. Not that there was anything very much for any of us to do, but it doesn't seem quite natural to make no movement at all.'

'That's interesting,' said the inspector.

'I've gone over it in my mind till I'm tired,' said Miss Hogg. 'All I can remember is he gave me a very nasty look when I told the Vicar I was now a private investigator. Of course, I can understand that now.'

'Just so.' The inspector pushed back his plate with a sigh of repletion. 'I shall have to see everybody again and ask them if they knew the bishop as Milligan. I'm just waiting first for the finger-print report. Professor Hoade didn't actually meet him yesterday, and there was no point in asking him to view the body when we thought it was the bishop. But now he may turn out to be somebody in his own line.'

'I suppose Professor Hoade is above suspicion?' asked Miss Hogg.'

'Nobody is,' said the inspector shortly. He got up, and put his chair back carefully under the table. 'Well, that was lovely grub,' he said. 'Thank you very much. I wish I could stay, but I must get back to the treadmill.'

'If you have time, do give us a ring in the morning,' Miss Hogg urged him.

'Certainly,' said the inspector.

But his ring came much earlier, in fact it was barely eight o'clock when the telephone rang in the office.

'Inspector Bruce here,' he said. 'The Vesseys have decamped. Went off in the car this afternoon, and took luggage with them. Mr. Vessey was driving.'

'Do you know where they've gone?'

'Not yet, but we shall by morning. Looks as if they're in a panic, doesn't it?'

'I don't know,' said Miss Hogg. 'It might be a long-standing engagement.'

'Long-standing my foot!' exclaimed the inspector. 'They haven't even cancelled their milk, because I've been through to the dairy. And their daily woman didn't know a thing about it.'

'I just can't accept Mrs. Vessey as a murderer,' said Miss Hogg. 'By the way, what about our third American on the Green?'

'Shumacher? I'm seeing him tomorrow. There's no connection with Miss Emily or Milligan that I can see.'

'His manservant would make a perfect murderer,' said Miss Hogg. 'I suppose that ought really to rule him out. I wish I could think of some excuse to interview him.'

'Don't stick your neck out,' warned the inspector. 'They may not have finished yet.'

'Oh, I don't think they have,' agreed Miss Hogg.

'Well, I should go to bed early tonight if I were you, and make up for last night.'

'I will,' said Miss Hogg demurely, and as the inspector rang off she reflected that she had never told him about the pebbles.

They spent an hour by the fire in the back room before going to bed. In the cupboard under the stairs Miss Hogg had found an old lampshade from which she removed the remains of the silk, and with some gold-coloured silk cord she had once thought to use as piping on a dressing-gown until she found it was too thin, she fixed the four parchment pages from the Monkey Brand tin on to the wire frame, Milly helping to punch the holes round the four edges of each page. It only took them a little over half an hour, but the result was not very satisfactory.

'Not very glamorous, is it?' asked Miss Hogg. 'There must be some sort of knack about it we haven't got. It doesn't seem right where the pages join together.'

'There may be a book about it in the library,' suggested Milly.

Miss Hogg gave an enormous yawn.

'We'll just see what it looks like on the lamp,' she said.

There was a small lamp with a Chinese-patterned shade standing on top of the case of an old-fashioned sewing-machine which had belonged to Miss Hogg's mother. Milly took out the bulb, unscrewed the ring which held the shade in position, and then put on the parchment shade they had just made. Then she put in the bulb and pressed the switch. They were rewarded by a mournful, brownish light.

'It must be the wrong kind of parchment,' said Miss Hogg, with another prodigious yawn. 'Leave it, Milly, and we'll go to bed.'

CHAPTER 18

On the Thursday morning the inspector went through the reports on his desk at an early hour. There had been no difficulty about finding the Vesseys. They had driven straight down to Brighton, and were staying at the Crown and Anchor, a small and rather exclusive hotel just off the front. Even more important, the hotel had been located where Milligan had spent the week-end. It was the Brontë in Bernard Street, just off Russell Square. There were two large suit-cases, which were being held at New Scotland Yard.

The inspector was on the point of leaving for Westminster when he was told the Superintendent would like to see him.

'They want you at New Scotland Yard, my lad,' said the Superintendent, when he poked his head in at the door. 'The Assistant Commissioner himself wants to see you. And in your private ear I may tell you that M.I.5 are on to this job of yours for some reason.'

'Military Intelligence, sir?' The inspector was startled.

'Don't ask me anything about it,' returned the Superintendent. 'I'm just a bloody office boy. The A.C. may reveal all to you, though I doubt it, but the only thing I know is they're checking up on all the American residents in South Green.'

'I see,' said the inspector, and went thoughtfully back to his office.

Before leaving for the Yard, he rang Miss Hogg to enquire if there had been any development at her end. He told her about the Vesseys, and added: 'I'm leaving them alone for the moment. What seems more important is we've found the hotel where Milligan spent Saturday and Sunday nights. It's the Brontë in Bernard Street. I'm going there when I've been to Scotland Yard.'

'I've a feeling we're going to get somewhere soon,' said Miss Hogg cheerfully.

'There's one thing that emphasizes the American angle,' said the inspector. There were really two, but he must not mention M.I.5. 'I looked all over the path and the flower-beds at the Laurels early this morning, and I found a Camel in a clump of berberis in front of the library window.'

'A *camel*!' exclaimed Miss Hogg.

'It's an American brand of cigarette,' explained the inspector. 'It was hardly smoked at all. Just lighted and then stubbed out. I think the fellow who smoked it had been keeping a watch in the bushes.'

'Well, good hunting,' said Miss Hogg. She did not tell him that a plan for the day had burst upon her like a revelation while he had been speaking.

Assistant Commissioner Lamb might have been any Under-Secretary from any of the buildings on the other side of Whitehall. He looked the perfect Civil Servant, quietly dressed, of medium height, with dark hair greying at the temples, and nothing but a certain unobtrusive air of authority to make you look twice at him. He was a church-warden in his home suburb, which was Wimbledon, and kept a mistress in Balham.

He greeted Inspector Bruce as if they were old friends, though actually they had never met before. Apart from deaths on the road, described in the ritual formula: 'The deceased pedestrian came into collision with a motor vehicle driven by . . .' there had been no case of homicide in South Green since it had been incorporated in the Metropolitan Police Area.

'We've had a transatlantic call, as I expect they've told you,' he said. He pushed a carton of cigarettes across the desk. 'It seems this Milligan was a well-known character, and they're still interested in him. His main stamping ground was San Francisco, and then he moved to Chicago, where he ran various gambling rackets until a year or two ago, when the gang seemed to break up. Have a cigarette, Inspector.'

'Thank you, sir. Then it's quite definite he's Milligan.'

'Oh, yes, it was Milligan. They recognized his prints all right. You know,' said the A.C., 'they have more than fourteen million finger-prints at Hoover's place in Washington. I once went over their Training College at Quantico. It's remarkably unlike Hendon. But then our problems are different.'

The inspector lit his cigarette, and tried to make suitable noises to indicate appreciation and agreement.

'There were two other members of the gang,' went on the A.C. He consulted a pad on the desk in front of him. 'Dough Face and Bonelli.'

'Dough Face?'

'A sobriquet, I imagine. Probably a very pasty complexion. These Americans will take their pleasures at drug stores, Inspector. And they have quite a passion for iced water.' The Assistant Commissioner shuddered. 'But Bonelli is described as almost a gentleman. He had a College education – which actually need not mean a great deal in America. You could equate it with the Grammar School type over here. Nothing has been heard of Dough Face and Bonelli for nearly three years.'

'They may be over here, then?'

'Highly likely,' agreed the Assistant Commissioner. 'It's not only dollars we get from America.'

'Milligan ran a gambling racket, you say?'

The Assistant Commissioner referred again to the pad in front of him.

'Gambling saloons – joints, I think they are called over there – was what first brought them to the notice of the authorities. But they seem to have branched out, and had quite a number of irons in the fire. They were suspected of having a hand in several jewel robberies, and Dough Face is known to have been implicated in the sale of a fraudulent Old Master.'

The inspector pricked up his ears.

'That almost ties up with Sir Arthur Dewdney,' he said. 'Only his speciality was manuscripts. You wouldn't think there'd be much of a market for them.'

'Oh, but I expect there is. Collectors are quite mad, and will pay almost anything for something they think is unique. What they want is something no one else has got.'

'I've known some pretty mad stamp collectors,' said the inspector.

'There's another thing,' said the A.C. 'Milligan used to have a wife. She'd been a small-part actress in a touring company before he married her. She walked out on him some years ago, and nothing is known about her since. She probably got a job entertaining the troops, came to England, and remained here.'

'It doesn't seem to link up with Sir Arthur Dewdney and Miss Emily's library,' said the inspector.

'No, it doesn't. But I'm just giving you all the facts I've had given to me. You must make what you can of them. By the way, Vessey, the painter fellow, rang up the Home Secretary yesterday.'

'He told me he was going to,' said the inspector.

'Said the police had been persecuting his wife. Well, the old boy doesn't interfere in that sort of thing. He merely rang up the Deputy Commissioner and told him about it, and it was passed on to me.'

The inspector recounted his interview with the Vesseys, and the reason for his visit.

'I can hardly imagine Vessey or his wife are after your Dewdney manuscript,' said the A.C. 'They must have plenty of money. I was astounded to hear the other day he gets £500 for a portrait. Only about five by four,' he added. 'I sometimes wish I'd been gifted. It's damn difficult to make both ends meet these days.' Particularly, he reflected, when young ladies in Balham have developed such expensive tastes.

'Five by four,' exclaimed the inspector. 'It's £25 a square foot.'

'And barely takes him a week,' said the A.C. 'Well, be careful of him, but you needn't worry about this end. We shall back you up, of course.'

There was a pause, and the inspector was preparing to take his leave, when the Assistant Commissioner said:

'There's one more thing, but it may be important. It's quite unofficial, but M.I.5 are interested.'

'I had already heard that they were enquiring into the Americans in South Green, sir.'

'The F.B.I. are definitely interested in this Milligan from the espionage point of view. But the oddest thing is this, we had an enquiry from them about Sir Arthur Dewdney and any surviving relatives before ever this Milligan murder took place. In fact it was a week ago today. Of course neither Sir Arthur nor Miss Emily Dewdney had or have any kind of police record, and so we informed them.' The A.C. pursed up his lips. 'As you know, Military Intelligence does not confide very much in the Metropolitan Police. They prefer to work on their own. But if you see a glamorous Mata Hari on the Green, or a mysterious character in a false beard, don't be too quick at arresting them. It may be a colonel from M.I.5.' The Assistant Commissioner laughed heartily. Military Intelligence was one of his *bêtes noires*. 'We shall back you up.'

The inspector took this as a sign of dismissal, and got to his feet.

'By the way,' said the A.C., 'her name was Monica Potts.'

'Mrs. Vessey?' asked the inspector, somewhat bewildered at this information.

'No, Mrs. Milligan. She may crop up, you know.'

CHAPTER 19

'IF anyone can get anything out of Mrs. Vessey,' remarked Miss Hogg to her friend Milly, as she came back from the telephone after the inspector had rung off, 'then it could be me. I mean,' she explained, 'there's a chance she might open up to a fellow-woman where she wouldn't to a policeman, even a nice one like the inspector.'

She glanced without flinching at the fellow-woman in the mirror over the kitchen-cum-dining-room mantelpiece. She was used to the somewhat shapeless tweed suit, a bargain at the winter sales two years before, the not very alluring hair style based on two main ideas, that it must not get into her eyes and must not require any first aid from getting-up to bedtime, and the piercing grey eyes behind the rimless pince-nez. It did not strike her that in uniform she would have resembled almost any man's conception of the prototypal policewoman. A faint doubt may have shot through her mind for she turned to Milly and said:

'You must come, too. It's easier to sit about and seize an opportunity when there are two of you.'

'Where is it we have to go?' asked Milly, all of a flutter.

'Brighton. We'll get the eleven o'clock if we start in half an hour, and be there at twelve. They're at the Crown and Anchor.'

The Crown and Anchor which was some twenty yards from the Promenade up a side turning near the Southdown bus park, proved to be one of those exclusive little hotels which are owned by retired members of the theatrical, boxing and allied professions. The lounge and restaurant on the ground floor were open to the public, according to a discreet notice just inside the front door, and at twenty minutes past noon, Miss Hogg marched into the lounge with the air if

135

not with the panache of an army with banners, and demanded two gins and orange for herself and her friend. Here they sat under a potted palm, in rather uncomfortable wicker chairs, while Miss Hogg tried to think what her next move ought to be.

And here she had an amazing piece of luck. Detective work without flair is a matter of routine little different from any other kind of work, but without luck it is a weariness and vexation of spirit. Miss Hogg had been born lucky. No sixth sense but sheer luck had kept her from opening her desk on the occasion when the Fifth Form had imprisoned a white mouse in it. If she had done she would almost certainly have made an exhibition of herself. (It had been left to the maths mistress to do this when she absent-mindedly raised the lid to look for chalk in the course of the next period.) Sheer luck had given her the boundary stroke which won the Staff v. School match only last year (due to her glasses falling off just as the ball left the bowler's hand, and her blind swipe taking the ball dead in the centre of the bat). The only time her luck had failed her was when she sat on the cobbler's wax and ruined her skirt. But in a way, that had been lucky, too, for the girl who did it had been so contrite and worked so hard at French for the rest of the term that she had gained a distinction in the Leaving Certificate to the astonishment of the whole Common Room.

On this occasion, as Miss Hogg was trying to attract the attention of the extremely blasé waiter who had retired to the other end of the lounge, and was gazing out of the window at a blank wall the more completely to dissociate himself from them, a woman emerged from a door marked Private, and crossed the lounge in the direction of the door marked Coffee Room. She glanced across at them as she passed, stopped in her tracks, and then came over with out-stretched hand.

'I declare,' she said. 'It's Hogg. And Milly Brown.'

'Goodness!' exclaimed Miss Hogg. 'It's Beryl – Beryl Mortimer.'

'Beryl Monkton now. I married Leslie Monkton, the impresario, you know. And now we've got this place.'

'What a wonderful thing a university education is,' said Miss Hogg. 'It gives you friends everywhere. Do sit down and have a drink with us. As a matter of fact you may be able to help us.'

'I must just see everything is all right in the dining-room,' said Mrs. Monkton, 'and then I'll come back. You must have this one on me.' She signalled the waiter, who was now all attention. 'Gin and orange? Three gins and orange, Charles, and tell Jock to book them up to me.'

She was back in a few minutes, the waiter obsequiously drawing up a chair for her.

'Here's how,' she said. 'What do you want help over?'

'You have some people called Vessey staying,' said Miss Hogg. 'It's no good trying to get out of it, because I had it from the police.'

'The police!' exclaimed Mrs. Monkton. 'Whatever do you mean, Hogg? What could the police have to do with Mrs. Vessey? She's an old friend of mine.'

'That makes it all the better,' said Miss Hogg. 'I suppose you've read in the papers about the South Green murder?'

'Of course I have. But you don't mean to tell me it's got anything to do with Mrs. Vessey, because I just shouldn't believe you.'

'The whole point is she knows something about the man who was murdered. I was there when she ran into him.' And Miss Hogg proceeded to give an account of the meeting on Monday night between the bogus bishop and Mrs. Vessey.

Mrs. Monkton looked hard at her.

'You never were one for romancing, Hogg, I will say that,' she remarked when the recital was finished. Her glance took in the hair style, the pince-nez and the shapeless tweeds. 'I just don't understand it. I suppose there must be something in it, but it seems a lot of nonsense to me. There's one thing I would bank on, and that is that Monica Vessey never got herself mixed up in a murder. I've known her ever since she came to England at the end of the war – she was in a concert party run by the American Forces, and then she joined one of my husband's companies. When he packed up and we took this place she came down to stay with us, and it was here she met Vessey.'

'She knows something,' reiterated Miss Hogg, 'and the police have simply got to find out what it is. If they can eliminate her, she won't hear any more from them. But you do see, don't you, that in a case of murder they've got to follow up every clue, no matter who the person is?'

'What I don't see, Hogg, is what you've got to do with it.'

'It's my new profession,' said Miss Hogg, quite unabashed. She rummaged in her handbag, and produced one of her new cards, slightly bent at the corners.

'Private Investigator! You always were a case, Hogg. Wasn't she, Milly? I thought you were teaching.'

'I've given it up. And this is my first case. All I want to know is whether Mrs. Vessey has any information about this man Milligan.'

Mrs. Monkton looked up from her gin and orange with a startled expression.

'Did you say Milligan, Hogg?'

'That's the name of the man who was pretending to be a bishop, and got murdered.'

'Well, I must say that's very peculiar.' Mrs. Monkton put down her glass. 'Mrs. Vessey was in one of my husband's touring companies as I told you – she was very good at character parts – and do you know the name she acted under?'

'Spit it out,' Miss Hogg urged her inelegantly.

'It was Monica Milligan.'

'Then she must be a relation. You can see the police will be on her like a ton of bricks. If I could get her to tell me everything, then I might be able to save her a lot of trouble.'

'I'll tell you what I'll do,' said Mrs. Monkton, getting up and smoothing down her dress. 'I'll go up and ask her to come and have a drink in my sitting-room before lunch. Then I'll tell her more or less what you've told me, and see what she says. If she won't see you, I can't force her. But in any case you must have lunch on the house.'

It was ten minutes later that a middle-aged woman in a blue dress with white collar and cuffs came out of the door marked Private and across to their table. 'I'm the house-keeper,' she said in a pleasant Scots voice. 'Which of you two ladies is Miss Hogg?'

Miss Hogg revealed her identity.

'You come from Inverness?' she said.

'From Turriff,' replied the other. 'And you are no' English.'

'I come from Stirling.'

'That's good. Well, Mrs. Monkton says will you come upstairs. She's in her private sitting-room.'

'I'll stay down here, Hogg,' said Milly quickly. 'She'll be more likely to talk if there's only you.'

Miss Hogg followed the housekeeper through the door by which she had entered the lounge. It opened on two cor-ridors at right angles. The one on the left ended in the kitchens, for Miss Hogg had a glimpse of a fat man in white crowned with a chef's hat, and just before the kitchen was a swing door through which waiters were madly dashing to and fro calling out incomprehensible orders. The right-hand corridor, along which were several doors, all of them shut, ended in a staircase up which they went. The corridor above was carpeted and led up to a green baize door, no doubt giving on the main part of the hotel. Just before it was another door on which the housekeeper knocked, and then stood aside for Miss Hogg to enter.

Mrs. Vessey was sitting, small and shrinking, in an arm-chair at the side of the fireplace. Mrs. Monkton was mixing a cocktail over by the window.

'I've told Monica she'd better spill the beans,' said Mrs. Monkton as Miss Hogg came into the room. 'I've explained to her that if she doesn't, she'll probably have to tell the whole story in court, and then it'll be in all the papers, which is just what she's been trying to avoid, though going, as far as I can see, exactly the wrong way about it.'

'I don't know why that horrible man wanted to come to South Green of all places,' said Mrs. Vessey.

'What horrible man?' asked Miss Hogg.

'Why, Milligan. And all dressed up like a clergyman. It just bowled me over.'

'Milligan,' repeated Miss Hogg. 'But how did you know he was called Milligan?'

Mrs. Vessey looked miserably up at Mrs. Monkton who had come across with the drinks.

'You better make a clean breast of it, ducks,' said Mrs. Monkton. 'Have a glass of mother's ruin, and you'll feel like a new woman.'

Mrs. Vessey took the glass from her, and essayed a tentative sip. Then she straightened up rather abruptly. 'It's awfully strong,' she said.

Of course it is,' agreed Mrs. Monkton. 'It's one of my husband's inventions. He calls it Viper's Delight.'

'You were going to tell me why you knew he was called Milligan,' put in Miss Hogg.

Mrs. Vessey looked up at Mrs. Monkton and then across at Miss Hogg.

'I was once Mrs. Milligan,' she said miserably.

Miss Hogg had put down her glass and now took off her pince-nez and began to polish them on her handkerchief.

'Did Mr. Vessey know about it?'

'He didn't, but he does now.' Mrs. Vessey took another sip of her cocktail. 'You see, I went out to Hollywood in the stupid way girls do, and I was absolutely no good. In the end I got a sort of chorus part in a night spot, and it was there I met Milligan. He didn't seem a bad sort in some ways, and he was very generous, and quite the gentleman. In the end I married him. It seemed to be the best way out of Holly-wood. I didn't know at all where he got the dollars from until after I'd married him, and then I found he expected me to help him in all sorts of ways. . . .' Her voice died away. Miss Hogg and Mrs. Monkton said nothing. 'So I got a Reno divorce,' she went on, 'and then when I came over here I met Roger. I didn't know whether the divorce counted in England, so I pretended I was single, and got married in my maiden name. I'd been acting as Monica Milligan because it sounded better than Potts, but I told Roger it was just a stage name.'

Miss Hogg had been thinking.

'Is there anything wrong about a Reno divorce?' she asked.

'Our Supreme Court gave a ruling last year,' said Mrs. Vessey, 'that a quick divorce could be upset if the papers hadn't been served on the other party within the State in which the divorce was obtained. I don't know much about the law, but it seemed to me Milligan could have got the whole thing washed out, and then I should have been a bigamist.'

'But he hadn't written to you about it?'

'I just had never heard from him since the day I went to Reno, and that's nearly seven years ago. I didn't think he'd ever be able to trace me. And then I suddenly came on him on Monday night. I nearly died of fright.'

'Did you tell your husband when you got back?'

'I had to. He knew something had happened. I told him the whole thing. He didn't say anything very much, but told me not to worry, and he was sure it was all right. He said if Milligan tried any funny business he'd shoot him like a dog.' Even as she said it she shrank back into the chair, putting her hand to her mouth like a frightened child. 'Of course he didn't really mean it. He wouldn't hurt a fly.'

'In any case, he wasn't shot, he was brained with a pair of fire-tongs,' said Miss Hogg.

'And in any case,' she said to Milly over lunch, 'I don't see how Vessey could possibly know Milligan was going to the Laurels. If you ask me, that's a crucial point.'

CHAPTER 20

B<small>ACK</small> at Victoria Station in the late afternoon, they had a coffee in the Golden Arrow Bar. Having experienced all the excitement of action, Miss Hogg did not feel like sitting back, and waiting for the inspector to find her more clues. The blood of her Stirling forebears was now eagerly coursing through her veins, and ancient war cries resounding in her inner ear. A further plan was already formulated in her mind.

'It won't worry you if I don't come back with you tonight?' she asked Milly, who was gazing speculatively at the cakes under a glass cover on the counter.

'N – no,' replied Milly rather dubiously. 'Whatever are you going to do, Hogg?'

'I thought I'd stay a night at the Brontë Hotel, but don't say anything to the inspector if he happens to drop in. He might think I was interfering. But it struck me I might be able to get something out of the chambermaid where a man wouldn't. If there's anything to get, of course. And then I can go to the Science Museum in the morning. I brought those stones in my bag for if we got back in time to go there this afternoon, but I think museums shut at five, and it's too late today. I'll do it in the morning.'

'I shall be quite all right,' said Milly.

'There's some cherry brandy in the sideboard cupboard,' said Miss Hogg. 'And there's the cold chicken to finish up. Or you could make yourself an omelet.'

'What do I say if anyone rings up?'

'I'll ring the inspector myself when I've seen you to the train. I don't expect anyone else will ring up, but if they do, you can just say I'm out, and I'll be back about midday tomorrow.'

143

Having seen Milly to the entrance of the underground, rung the South Green police station and left a guarded message as the inspector was not in the building, she took the underground herself, changing at Charing Cross and Piccadilly Circus, and eventually emerged from the Russell Square tube station at the top of Bernard Street. On her left was the traffic flowing from the Kingsway to Euston and King's Cross; on her right, in the distance, the quiet of the Foundling Hospital. Turning right, she walked slowly down the street, scanning the fanlights of the houses opposite, for it was on the fanlights that most of them seemed to have their name painted. The Brontë was only a little way down, a not very prepossessing, but typical London house of the late Victorian period. Miss Hogg crossed over, hesitated whether to knock or ring, and finally, deciding that after all it was an hotel though not the sort to which she was accustomed, pushed open the door and entered.

The entrance hall, in which she found herself, seemed at first to be in almost total darkness. Such daylight as tried to filter through the opaque glass and grime of the front door gave up the struggle almost as soon as it crossed the threshold. A small bulb with a shade like an inverted saucer hanging from the dim recesses of the ceiling only served to emphasize the gloom, as if making darkness visible. The air was quite dead, and heavy with the smell of stale tobacco smoke and other even more unpleasant odours. As Miss Hogg's eyes grew more accustomed to the murky half-light, she became aware of a large Victorian hall-stand on which stood a dilapidated book in a shiny black cover. Fixed to the wall on either side of the hall-stand were two printed announcements, one headed 'Registration of Aliens', and the other a notice that the proprietor disclaimed all responsibility for any valuables left in the hotel.

A sudden thought struck Miss Hogg. She moved forward quickly, and turned the pages of the shiny black book. It was, as she had surmised, a somewhat primitive hotel register, and on the last page to record the names of visitors she saw the one she was looking for:

J. P. Milligan

The room number in the left-hand column was 5, the nationality was given as American, and the two columns for previous address and future destination had been left blank.

Even as she registered this information, a voice behind her said 'Can I help you?' It was a cold voice, with a bleak northern accent. Miss Hogg jumped, and closed the book quickly. Turning she was aware of an elderly man regarding her with what appeared to be a sinister expression, the more sinister because of a cast in his left eye. He appeared to have come from a door at the back of the hall.

' I – I wanted a room for tonight, please.'

'I don't know as we have one. I'll ask Mother.' A moment later and he had disappeared, almost as if he had dematerialized into the shadows.

'If he has a mother,' Miss Hogg thought to herself, 'she must be very near a hundred.'

The door at the back of the hall swung open, and this time a buxom young woman with a flowered apron over a cotton dress came into the hall from what was evidently the kitchen regions, for a strong smell of frying onions accompanied her.

'You wanting a room?' she asked. 'I'll bet the old man told you we hadn't any.'

'He did rather hint you were full up,' said Miss Hogg.

'Just like him. He hates anybody in the house. Says it's too much work for his wife. I could tell you who does the work round here,' she added, with a toss of her head. 'His wife's my aunt,' she went on, 'well, my aunt by marriage like. Her sister married my uncle, so it's a bit distant, you might say.'

'Then you have a room?'

'Half a dozen. Come up and have a look.' She turned at the stairs as a thought struck her. 'We don't do any meals except breakfast.'

'Oh, that's quite all right. I suppose I could have it about eight?'

'Eight to the tick, miss. I bring it up myself, see.'

'Thank you,' said Miss Hogg. 'By the way, what's your name? Mine's Flora Hogg.'

'They call me Rene, though I was christened Ireen.'

They had arrived at a landing even darker and stuffier than the hall. Rene had turned on a light, a replica of the one below, except that the shade in this case was green, and seemed to absorb most of the illumination. There were five doors, Miss Hogg was just able to discern, one of them marked Bathroom, one was blank, and the other three bore enamel numbers ranging from 3 to 5. The latter was opposite the stairs.

'We come from Haworth, miss, in Yorkshire. That's why they called it the Brontë. My granny used to remember old Mr. Brontë quite well, though she was chapel by rights.' Rene had paused at the top of the stairs to get her breath. 'Have you ever seen the Brontë films, miss?'

'I'm afraid I haven't,' said Miss Hogg. 'But I've read some of their books.'

'Ever so good they were,' said Rene. She went across and threw open the door of number 3. Miss Hogg caught a glimpse of an unmade bed, a pitch-pine wardrobe, and a window through which a grey light filtered from a sort of well.

'I must have forgot to do that one,' remarked Rene, unabashed, and quickly closing the door. She was about to try the next room when Miss Hogg said:

'What about 5? I should so like to be over the street, and I'm sure it must face the front.'

Rene looked momentarily disconcerted. She went to the banisters, peered down into the mephitic depths, and then came up to Miss Hogg and said in lowered tones:

'I didn't ought to tell you, miss. But we've had the police.'

'No,' breathed Miss Hogg, in what she hoped were suitably shocked tones.

'It happens now and again, as you might say, to the best houses, though I will say the boss is most particular. You might not think it, miss, but he gave you a good look over when you came in just now.' Miss Hogg could scarcely repress a shudder at the thought of that sinister glance giving her a good look over. 'Course he could see at once, miss, you weren't one of the young women we get trying it on sometimes.'

'And why did they come?' Miss Hogg tried to appear interested but not too interested, the sort of voice she had used when the Sixth Form tackled her about the private life of Verlaine.

Rene dropped her voice even lower.

'They came about the last person who was in number 5.'

'Indeed.'

Rene threw another glance over the banisters.

'Such a nice gentleman, he was. Jolly, you know. He was an American, but what was funny, he turned out to be a parson, too. I nearly died when I see him in his clergicals on the Sunday. The boss probably wouldn't have taken him in if he'd come first off in his clerical collar, but he wasn't wearing it when he came. You wouldn't believe what some of these clergymen are up to when they take rooms round here. The boss won't have them.'

147

Miss Hogg really did look a little shocked.

'And this was the room he had,' said Rene, throwing open the door of number 5.

It was certainly a nicer room than the one they had just caught a glimpse of. The bed was a large double one with walnut ends, there was a wardrobe of the same material, and a dressing-table, while in the corner to the left of the window was a washbasin with running water. The window itself was draped in lace curtains, a little grimy, but not excessively so considering the district, through which came the beams of the evening sun. After the landing, the room seemed quite light and airy.

'He went away on Monday, all dressed in his clericals,' went on Rene, continuing her saga. Obviously it was the most interesting thing that had happened in the house for a long time. 'And he never came back.' She dropped her voice again, but this time purely for effect. ''Course he'd paid in advance, the boss always sees to that, and he left two big suit-cases. Well, the next thing was the boss saw his photo in the paper. I never have time for a newspaper, myself, but the boss is a great reader. Takes the *Express* and the *Mirror* every day, and the *News of the World* and the *People* every Sunday. I read Lyndoe sometimes when I get back from chapel – I'm Taurus, you know, and my young man's Cancer. I've been a bit scared since I found out, because my father died of cancer, and he's bound to get it if it's in his stars.'

Miss Hogg felt a sensible word in season was indicated, but she was far more interested in the late occupant of number 5.

'It's a lot of nonsense,' she said. 'And what happened next?' she asked.

'Well, it turned out this chap had been murdered. What do you think of that, miss?' She glanced apprehensively round the room, as if the murderer might even now be lurking in the wardrobe, or under the bed.

'Goodness!'

'Not here, of course. Somewhere the other side of London. The boss thinks it's a person called Miss Emily Somebody who's done it, and he's a good one at weighing things up. It seems he had a secret randyvoo with her in the middle of the night at her house.'

Miss Hogg had seated herself on the bed, and was listening entranced.

'So you had the police round?'

'As soon as the boss saw this chap's picture in the paper yesterday, he knew it was him,' said Rene, throwing grammar and lucidity to the winds as she warmed to her narrative. 'And then he got an evening paper, which he doesn't do as a rule, and it said the police were anxious to get into touch with anyone who might know where he had been at the week-end, so he talked it over with my aunty, and in the end he rang up Scotland Yard. It's best to keep in with the police, even if it does make the neighbours talk,' said Rene, nodding her head sagely. She was standing at the foot of the bed, her hands clasped on the top of the walnut bed end.

'And then what happened?'

'Well, last night, almost as soon as he'd rung up, two coppers came round in a car. Ever so nice one of them was,' said Rene, appraising them in her mind's eye, 'though the other was a bit sarky, as if he knew all the answers before he asked you anything. They just had a look round, and then locked this door, and took the suit-cases away. And then this morning an inspector came. He hadn't a uniform on, but he showed the boss his card. He looked all round, but he could see there was nothing, and he asked if this chap had had any visitors, and then the boss asked him how long he was going to have to keep the room vacant, and he said there was no need if we wanted to use it as he'd done with it, and then he went away.'

'And did he? Have any visitors, I mean?'

'Well, the boss said not, miss, and I couldn't say, really, because Saturday's my night at the pictures – Stewart Grainger in *The Wrong Honeymoon*, ever so nice, it was. And on Sunday I go to chapel in the Tottenham Court Road. The boss wouldn't know, because he's always out playing snooker on a Saturday night, and on Sundays he and my aunty always listen to the play on the wireless, so they wouldn't hear anybody unless they knocked on the door in the hall. But I've thought of one thing since the inspector was here,' said Rene, opening her eyes wide. 'I brought him up a hot water bottle when I got back from chapel on Sunday night. You don't mind doing anything for anybody who's a real gentleman. And I remember now there was quite a smell of smoke in here. And I emptied some tab ends out of the ash-tray on Monday morning. You see,' she explained, 'I know he didn't smoke himself, because I noticed there wasn't an ash-tray when he took the room, and I got him one out of number 4, and he told me then he didn't smoke. I can't think why I didn't remember that before.' She gazed at Miss Hogg blankly. 'Do you think the police will have it in for me, miss, for tampering with the evidence?'

'I shouldn't think so,' said Miss Hogg. 'It's a pity you emptied the ash-tray.' She was just about to remark that she would pass the information on to the inspector, but she thought better of it. 'Well, I think I'll go out and get something to eat. Where's a good place?'

'There's a caff just up by the tube station,' replied Rene doubtfully. 'But you might prefer the Lyons' in Southampton Row. Is there anything else you want, miss?'

'No thank you, Rene. Just breakfast at eight.'

'It'll be twelve-and-six, miss, bed and breakfast. I have to get it in advance, or the boss would play pop. And will you write your name in the book downstairs before you go out? Now we've had the police round we shall have to be extra careful for a bit, the boss says.'

'Certainly,' said Miss Hogg. She took out her purse, and extracted a ten-shilling note and two half-crowns. 'One's for you,' she said, handing them over.

'Oh, thank you, miss. You can just knock on the far door downstairs if you want anything.'

When the girl had gone, Miss Hogg remained for a few moments seated on the bed, thinking. There was no evidence, that was clear. What there had been had vanished with Rene's tidying up. Her eye fell on the fireplace, in which was a large fan of what had once been white paper, but was now yellow with age and grey with dust.

'I wonder,' said Miss Hogg.

She got down on her knees in front of the hearth. At the bottom of the grate was a circular piece of ornamental work, with a brass knob in the centre, the vestigial descendant of what up north is known as a Tidy Betty. Miss Hogg pulled at the knob, and the curved piece of metal came away. It was as she had imagined, the debris of ages had been swept out of sight underneath the grate. There were the ends of twenty or thirty cigarettes, balls of hair and fluff, spent matches and bits of paper. Miss Hogg regarded this accumulation with distaste. Then she thrust in her hand. In the forefront, and quite fresh-looking, was a half-smoked cigarette, and the lettering on it was clear. It was a Camel.

CHAPTER 21

THE inspector, meanwhile, had not been idle. He had been through the late Mr. Milligan's luggage with, as his sergeant would describe it, 'a small tooth comb', but although it gave clear evidence of his identity, it did nothing more. There was no clue to indicate why he had come to England, and what was his motive in visiting South Green. Only one thing had struck the inspector as odd. The copy of the *Church Leader*, folded back to the page which contained the letter from the Vicar of South Green on the matter of aumbries was in one of the suit-cases, and the letter itself had been marked round with red ink. The inspector was aware that no pen containing red ink had been found on Milligan or in any of his cases. The particular issue was dated only eight days before the pseudo-bishop had landed at Southampton, and it was not a paper, the inspector reflected, that was of such importance its editions were likely to be flown across the Atlantic. All things considered, it was highly unlikely the paper had come into Milligan's possession before he landed in England, and it seemed more than probable that someone had handed it to him after his arrival. The boat-train had reached Waterloo just after 11 o'clock on the Saturday morning. This would have given Milligan less than two hours to purchase his clerical outfit, or, at least, the back-to-front collar and the purple stock. If he had not had a black suit with him, he could have got this in the afternoon, and it was hardly likely that he would get it at a clerical outfitters anyway. (The inspector, in common with the majority of his countrymen, had rather exaggerated ideas about clerical remuneration. He little knew that most incumbents below the rank of archdeacon have been reduced in the last quarter of a century to getting their clothes 'off the peg'.) What it all added up to was that Milligan had probably been met by an accomplice, and the scheme was all cut and dried at the time of his arrival.

The next thing the inspector did was to go through the complete notes of the case, including all the statements taken by his sergeant from the residents of Barbrook Drive. Everybody appeared to have been in bed and asleep at the material time on Tuesday night. Nobody had seen anything. Mr. Bartley Craig, who had offered the sergeant a sherry, which had been refused, had been desolated to be able to offer so little assistance, but he, too, so he affirmed, had been in bed and peacefully asleep by midnight. The sergeant had even interviewed the residents of Ormonde Court, but no one had heard anyone enter or leave the building after midnight. One old lady said she heard a car start up just after the church clock struck the half-hour – she was not absolutely sure it was half past midnight, it might have been half past eleven or, indeed, half past one, because she had just woken up and then fallen asleep again, but it had *felt* like half past midnight – but no one else in the building had heard it, or knew anything about it.

'Not that it's any use,' said the inspector gloomily. 'I can't see the murderer driving up to Miss Emily's in a car.'

'He may have parked a car somewhere near to make his getaway,' suggested the sergeant, a tall, dark young man, hag-ridden with the urge to get on.

'The getaway must have been about twenty minutes after the old lady heard the car – if she heard it at half past midnight. If it was any other time, it doesn't matter a damn. Hoade's got a car, but can you see him taking it out just to run round the Green and murder someone in Miss Emily's library, and then drive back to the flats?'

'I don't suppose the murderer was going to commit a murder until he got there,' said the sergeant.

'Then he wouldn't want to park his car somewhere for a getaway,' the inspector pointed out, 'if there was nothing to get away from. If the murderer came from South Green, even if he was only round at Miss Emily's to do a bit of breaking and entering, I can't see him drawing attention to himself by having a car on the job. If the chap came from London, then he wouldn't be starting the thing up from Ormonde Court at half after midnight.'

It was the sergeant's car, his only contribution of any substance, and he fought hard for it.

'He might have been calling on Hoade or Shumacher or some other resident on the Green before going round to Miss Emily's.'

'If he did, then he would have left the car parked wherever it was,' said the inspector irritably, 'and walked across. Anyway, it doesn't seem to lead us anywhere. I think we can wash it out.'

But the car came back into the picture only half an hour later.

At twenty minutes past two, Lord Hounslow rang up the police station. The only son of the late Chief Baron, he had been many years Chairman of the local Bench, and at one time had been a Deputy Lieutenant. Owing to increasing deafness, for he was approaching his eightieth year, he had, since the war, lived in a semi-retirement. His call was received by a young constable at the switchboard in the front office.

'Is that the South Green police station?'

'South Green police station, sir,' repeated the constable.

'I hope I'm not being charged for this call. I'm ringing up entirely as a matter of duty, in the public interest.'

The constable had pulled a pad towards him, and he now threw a helpless glance over his shoulder at the desk sergeant.

'Who is speaking, please?'

'Lord Hounslow, here. I dialled Whitehall 1212, but whoever I got on to told me to dial 999. If I'm charged for the calls I shall certainly have the matter raised in the House.'

'I'm sure you won't be charged, sir. Just one moment, sir.'

The sergeant was making frantic signs across the room. The constable placed a large red hand over the mouthpiece.

'What's all this about a charge?' asked the sergeant. 'You can't tell a person he won't be charged with an offence off your own bat. What's the fellow been doing?'

'It's the charge for the telephone call he's worrying about,' explained the constable. 'It's Lord Hounslow.'

'Oh, Lord Hounslow,' said the sergeant. Although as a magistrate he had never been able to hear much of the evidence, he had been noted for the soundness of his judgments, from the police point of view. Lately he had become rather a nuisance for he was always complaining about the cars parked on the Green outside his house, though it was more usual for him to rush out and tackle the constable on the beat.

The constable reverted to the telephone which was sputtering angrily.

'Sorry, sir,' he said.

'My lord,' prompted the sergeant.

'I'm sorry, my lord. Who do you wish to speak to?'

'It's about this murder.'

'Murder, sir! I mean, my lord.'

'This murder at Miss Emily Dewdney's. On Tuesday night,' added his lordship, as if to pin it down once and for all, so that it could not be confused with any other murders which might have taken place there. 'Scandalous thing. It might have been the death of the poor old lady. I don't know what things are coming to. I've got some evidence for what it's worth.'

155

'Hold on a minute, my lord. I'll put you through to the inspector in charge of the case.'

'I can't hear what you say, but I'm not going to repeat anything over the telephone. You never know who may be listening. And it isn't my evidence, it's a friend of mine. He's a philatelist.'

'A what, sir?' The constable had given up trying to take notes.

'A philatelist. Specializes in the West Indies. Foolish to my mind, because so many people specialize in them, and it makes them far too expensive. But that's neither here nor there. He's been having luncheon with me, and I'll keep him here until the inspector or someone comes round.' And Lord Hounslow rang off.

The constable mopped his brow, and rang through to Inspector Bruce. In three minutes the inspector was on his way to Adelaide Lodge, so called because Queen Adelaide had stayed there on one occasion while alterations were being affected at Kew Palace.

He was admitted by an elderly lady who occupied an ill-defined position somewhere between housekeeper to Adelaide Lodge and companion to Lady Hounslow. Her ladyship, although ten years younger than her husband, suffered from various forms of hypochondria – at the moment, owing to an article she had read in a *Digest*, she was indulging in a slipped disc, which sounded even more exciting than the fibrositis of the year before – but already the hounds of spring were baying up the bazaar-opening season, during which Lady Hounslow was in great demand by the various South London churches of the Evangelical persuasion, and during which, also, her health noticeably improved.

Lord Hounslow was in his study, a room which, probably because of its painted ceiling, was known as Queen

Adelaide's boudoir. Lady Hounslow never used any of the downstairs rooms, except the dining-room on formal occasions. Usually her meals were taken up on a tray to the first floor. With Lord Hounslow was a dried up little man of almost the same age, dressed in an old-fashioned knicker-bocker suit.

'Good afternoon, Inspector,' said Lord Hounslow. 'This is my friend, Mr. Mountjoy. He'll tell you his story. Might be important. He came to dinner on Tuesday night to go over my Gambia.'

'Gambia!' The inspector was momentarily disconcerted, wondering what on earth it was. Perhaps the man, Mountjoy, was a doctor.

'Gambia,' said Lord Hounslow impatiently. 'It's a colony in West Africa, of course, but that's neither here nor there. I shan't be charged for ringing you up, shall I?' he added abruptly.

'Certainly not, my lord.'

'That's good. We shall be bankrupt soon enough as it is. I don't know what the world's coming to.'

'This gentleman has some information?' asked the inspector, still addressing himself to Lord Hounslow.

'It's a rather shocking thing, Inspector. 'Pon my soul, I didn't know what to say when he told me. The Ordes are neighbours of ours. I've been there to dinner, and they've been here.'

The inspector took out his note-book.

'What you have to tell me relates to Sir Wellington Orde?' he asked.

'It's Mountjoy who saw him,' said Lord Hounslow. 'But I'll just explain, and then he can tell you his story. We had a late night on Tuesday. Went on from Gambia to Used Abroad. Fascinating, Inspector, but at my age you need a magnifying glass. Then we had a nightcap – quite a small one, Mr. Mountjoy is a very careful driver. And it was after midnight when he left here.'

'The church clock on the Green was just chiming the half-hour,' put in Mr. Mountjoy. He had a high-pitched voice, and seemed rather nervous.

'I see,' said the inspector, making a note of the time, and realizing instantly that it was the car that had been heard by the old lady in Ormonde Court.

There was a pause as Mr. Mountjoy looked at Lord Hounslow, and Lord Hounslow looked at Mr. Mountjoy.

'The thing is,' said Lord Hounslow, 'you can't prefer a charge after the event if you haven't any witnesses, can you?'

The inspector was puzzled.

'In what way, my lord? I'm afraid I don't quite follow.'

'Well, to make a clean breast of it, Mountjoy here went off without his lights. Forgot to switch them on. In fact he went half-way round the Green before he remembered them.'

'Yes, my lord.'

'You can't get him for that now, can you?' asked Lord Hounslow anxiously. 'I mean he's told you himself. And in the public interest,' he added.

'Oh, certainly not, my lord. He won't hear anything more about it.'

'That's all right, then,' said Lord Hounslow. 'Relieved your mind, eh, Mountjoy?'

'It was just an oversight,' said Mr. Mountjoy. 'The street lamps, that is the lamps round the Green, were still on, and I thought my sidelights were on until I turned the corner of East Side. And then, quite suddenly, all the lamps went out, and I realized they were off – my own lamps, I mean.'

'The Council extinguishes the lamps on the Green at half past midnight,' said Lord Hounslow. 'It's supposed to be an economy measure, though as they were out all the time throughout the war, you'd have thought they'd economized enough.'

The inspector was beginning to feel like someone groping his way through a fog.

'You mentioned Sir Wellington Orde,' he said. 'How exactly does he come into it?'

'Mountjoy saw him round at Miss Emily's.'

The inspector sat up with a jerk.

'Mr. Mountjoy saw him on Tuesday night?'

'That's what we're trying to tell you, Inspector. Tell him in your own words, Mountjoy.'

'Will I – will I have to give evidence, Inspector?'

'It depends, sir. If what you have to say leads to the apprehension of the murderer, then of course you would.'

'Oh dear,' said Mr. Mountjoy. He looked appealingly at Lord Hounslow. 'I'm not at all intimate with Sir Wellington, but I've had dinner with him.'

'Duty to the public,' said Lord Hounslow sternly. 'That's what you must bear in mind, Mountjoy. Duty to the public.'

'You met Sir Wellington Orde?' asked the inspector.

'I didn't actually meet him,' replied Mr. Mountjoy. 'I switched on my headlights, as I told you, just as I turned up East Side. And in the beam I saw Sir Wellington Orde.'

'You're quite sure it was Sir Wellington?'

'Oh, no doubt about it at all, not at all. I shouldn't have noticed him if he hadn't behaved in such a peculiar fashion.'

'How was that, sir?'

'I live at Richmond, Inspector, and I generally go back by the river as it's quieter, which means turning down Barbrook Drive, instead of going along the London road. I must have been about twenty yards away from the turning when I switched the headlights on, and there was Sir

Wellington, right ahead of me. He – he simply jumped into a drive gate, and disappeared.'

'Would you be able to identify the gate?'

'Oh, it was Miss Emily's. No doubt at all. The house on the far corner hasn't a gate on to the Green, so Miss Emily's is the first gate from the corner.'

'He thought nothing about it, of course,' put in Lord Hounslow, who had been listening to this exchange somewhat impatiently. 'But yesterday it was in all the evening papers about the murder. He telephoned me as soon as he read about it. I told him he'd better come to luncheon today and I'd ring you up. In the public interest,' concluded Lord Hounslow.

'I shouldn't like to get Sir Wellington into trouble,' said Mr. Mountjoy.

'What I can't understand,' said Lord Hounslow, 'is what the Vicar was doing to have the fellow stay with him. I see in this morning's paper he wasn't a bishop at all. It seems to me a very peculiar thing for a Vicar to have a fellow staying with him masquerading as a bishop.'

The inspector, rather pusillanimously, felt it was not up to him to resolve this difficulty.

'Could I have your full name and address, sir?' he said, turning to Mr. Mountjoy. 'I may have to communicate with you again. And I shall have to take a statement from Sir Wellington Orde.'

CHAPTER 22

Miss Hogg spent an uneventful night at the Brontë Hotel, though she locked the door and looked in the wardrobe and under the bed before finally settling down for the night. She had been going to have a bath, but decided against it on inspecting the bathroom, which Rene had obviously been too busy to clean out for some days.

The next morning she breakfasted in bed, a thing which, she reflected, was becoming almost a habit in her new profession. Rene brought her up two sausages and some fried potatoes, four slices of bread and a small pat of butter, a saucer with some marmalade in the middle of it, and a pot of good strong tea. She confided in Miss Hogg that she had had an egg for her, but it had seemed a bit off when she broke it.

'So Aunty's giving it to the boss,' she concluded. 'He never notices what he has to eat, and it's a shame to waste it.'

In the morning light, the proprietor did not seem half so sinister. He had shrunk to his normal stature as the proprietor of a third-rate Bloomsbury hotel. He met her in the hall as she came down, and wished her good morning. The door had been propped back with a brass door-stopper, and it was possible to see quite clearly.

'Did she tell you we'd had a murder at the weekend?' he asked.

Miss Hogg rightly gathered that by the feminine pronoun he was referring to his niece by marriage once removed.

'She mentioned it,' she said guardedly, not wanting to get Rene into trouble.

'He wasn't murdered here, of course, but this was the last place he stayed in,' said the old man, his eyes gleaming.

'His last night on earth it was. Or his last night but one,' he added, in the interest of strict accuracy.

'How exciting,' said Miss Hogg. It was all she could think of to say on the spur of the moment.

The old man's left eye swivelled round, almost as if endowed with a life of its own, and he tapped her on the arm with a skinny forefinger.

'I told Rene not to breathe a word about it, so as not to disturb your rest. But that room you had was *his* room.' An expression of ghoulish enjoyment spread over the old man's face.

'How dreadful!' exclaimed Miss Hogg. She hoped she sounded suitably impressed. 'Well, I have to get to South Kensington, so I must be off. Say good-bye to Rene for me.'

It was just 11 o'clock when she got to the Science Museum. By mistake she had gone first to the Victoria and Albert. She marched up the steps not knowing what department she should ask for, but the matter was settled for her by a uniformed attendant. His eye took her in from head to foot. Her shoes had not been cleaned for at least two days. Obviously she was a scientist.

'The Geiger Counter demonstration is on the first floor,' he said. 'At the end of the corridor on your right at the top of the stairs.'

'Is that the Physics section?' she asked.

'That's right, madam. The demonstration is just beginning.'

Miss Hogg had not the remotest idea what Geiger Counters were, but she went up the stairs and turned to the right as directed. If it were a scientific demonstration she would surely be able to ask someone about the stones. The first floor was more like a vast hall than a corridor, and glass cases containing every conceivable kind of apparatus were in evidence on all sides. At the farther end were a group of people, all of them male, including two Indians, a Negro, and several schoolboys. A man with flowing white hair and a white walrus moustache was standing on a small platform, evidently put there for the occasion, and holding up a curious sort of instrument which looked to Miss Hogg as if it were a cross between a portable wireless set and an early vacuum cleaner. On a table at his side were a number of other equally odd-shaped boxes.

As Miss Hogg approached, the instrument the man was holding, and which appeared to be pointing directly at her, suddenly came to life.

'Tock – tock – tock!'

'Good God!' exclaimed the man with the white hair, nearly dropping the thing, and recovering it by the skin of his teeth. It was obvious that something quite unrehearsed was taking place.

Miss Hogg, wondering if it were some kind of time bomb, which surely they would de-fuse before it actually exploded, went a little nearer and peered at the thing through her pince-nez. On which the box began to tick away like an agitated alarm-clock, but with a sort of sinister undercurrent that was somehow rather frightening.

'Tock - tock - tock - tock - tock!'

'My God, the woman's radio-active!' exclaimed the man with the white hair.

The group which had closed in round Miss Hogg fell back, with every expression of alarm, all except the schoolboys who came closer, with looks of pleasurable anticipation on their faces.

'Bad medicine,' said the Negro, whom fear had evidently transported straight back to the jungle.

'She's emitting gamma rays,' said one of the Indians.

'It may be a luminous watch,' said his companion.

'Tock - tock - tock - tock - tock!'

A tall thin man with a hatchet face, in blue serge that had an aura of officialdom about it, came from the other side of the platform and touched Miss Hogg on the shoulder.

'You'd better come with me,' he said. It was a cultured voice, but it had a steely ring.

'I wanted to see the Keeper,' said Miss Hogg. 'Or one of his assistants.'

'Come with me,' repeated the man in blue serge. He waved a hand to the demonstrator who was still standing thunder-struck in the middle of the platform. 'I'll deal with this, Homer,' he said. 'Carry on.' And he led Miss Hogg to a door at the end of the hall.

'By the way,' he said, as he threw open the door and motioned her through on to a stone-floored landing, with a spiral staircase leading upwards to the left and downwards to the right, 'you are not suffering from cancer, are you?'

Miss Hogg was on the point of replying 'I was born under Taurus', but something in the man's eye deterred her.

'I hardly think so,' she said. 'I've no knowledge of it.'

'Sorry. I had to ask. It struck me that in some extraordinary way you might have had a needle left in you. You'd be surprised the things that can happen under this new Health Act.'

He had preceded her up the spiral staircase to the left, and now they had reached another door, similar to the one on the floor below. Her companion opened this, revealing a passage running the length of the building, down which they proceeded at a brisk pace. Half-way down they stopped at a more resplendent door in polished mahogany, on which her escort tapped. A voice could be heard bidding them enter.

The room they entered was a large and comfortably furnished office. At a very large desk placed in front of the window sat a very small man, his face almost entirely obscured by an outsize pair of horn-rimmed spectacles.

164

'I'm sorry to disturb you, Director, but it's an urgent security matter.' Miss Hogg's companion closed the door carefully. 'What is your name, young woman?'

'Miss Hogg.'

'And your address?'

Miss Hogg was beginning to feel angry. She felt it was time someone explained things to her.

'What is all this about?' she asked. 'I merely came here to get some information –'

'Quite, quite, quite. My name is Colonel Brassett. This is the Director, Sir Hamilton Tuke. I hope we shan't have to detain you very long.' Colonel Brassett turned to the Director. 'Professor Burbage is in the building, sir. I think we'd better get him.'

The Director took up a telephone and spoke into it. Colonel Brassett drew up a chair and motioned Miss Hogg to be seated. When the Director had finished giving instructions into the telephone there was silence for a few moments as they looked at Miss Hogg. Her mind had gone back to the times when she used to send girls up to the headmistress. Not very often, for she was a good disciplinarian, but it had had to be done occasionally.

There came a tap on the door, and a youngish man with tousled hair falling over his forehead opened it and put his head in.

'You wanted me, Director?'

'Come in, come in,' said the Director. 'I think you know Colonel Brassett. This is a Miss Hogg who attended the demonstration this morning. I think the colonel wants your advice.'

Professor Burbage shambled into the room, rather like an angular grizzly, and took a chair which the colonel had placed at the side of the Director's desk.

'As the Director has told you, this young lady attended the Geiger Counter demonstration in the Physics section

165

this morning,' the colonel explained. 'And she's carrying radio-active material on her person. Homer was going to demonstrate with a small quantity of some isotope, but the Geiger Counter reacted like mad as soon as this lady came near the platform.'

'You aren't carrying any active isotopes around with you, are you?' the Professor asked Miss Hogg.

'I don't even know what they are,' said Miss Hogg crossly. 'I took modern languages,' she added wildly.

The Professor looked rather helplessly at the Director, and then both of them looked at the colonel.

'You are certainly carrying something to which a Geiger Counter reacts,' said Colonel Brassett decisively. 'Have you no idea what it can be?'

'I came here,' said Miss Hogg, opening her bag and taking out the canvas sack containing the Transcaucasian cure for rheumatism, 'to ask what these stones were.' She got up and emptied the contents of the canvas receptacle on to the desk in front of the Director.

'Good heavens!' exclaimed the Professor. 'Pitchblende.'

'My dear young lady,' said the colonel, 'where did you get this stuff from?'

'It came from Sir Arthur Dewdney's, that is to say from Miss Emily's, but it was in her father's luggage.'

This was evidently Greek to the Director and Professor Burbage, but the colonel was still in command of the situation.

'Look,' he said. 'I must know exactly who you are and where you come from. I take it you live in South Green?'

Miss Hogg was past feeling surprise at this question.

'My father was Superintendent of Police at South Green,' she said. 'He died in January. I used to teach at the County Girls' School, but now I'm a private investigator, which is how I came into contact with Miss Emily Dewdney. You

166

can ring up the South Green police,' she added. 'They know me well. The present Superintendent used to play chess with my father.'

'May I use your phone, Director?' asked Colonel Brassett.

'Certainly, certainly.' The Director pushed the instrument over.

Miss Hogg heard him ask for an exchange which sounded like 'Treasury', but her attention was taken by Professor Burbage.

'These stones, as you call them,' he said, poking them with his finger, 'are from an extremely rich deposit of uranium.'

'I thought they might be lead,' said Miss Hogg.

'Lead is, you might say, the dead end, and uranium the live one,' said Professor Burbage.

Colonel Brassett turned from the telephone and said:

'I have Superintendent Frazer on the line here. Would you speak to him, Miss Hogg? Purely for identification purposes.'

Miss Hogg took the receiver which he held out to her, and said 'Hullo!' into the mouthpiece.

A voice which she recognized immediately as the Superintendent's said:

'Is that Miss Flora?'

'I wish you'd tell me what this is all about.'

'Would you give me your father's two Christian names?' asked the Superintendent.

'Charles James,' replied Miss Hogg.

'Good enough. And who was his favourite author?'

'Cobbett,' said Miss Hogg, without any hesitation.

'Put me on to the colonel again,' said the Superintendent at the other end. 'By the way, there's been a spot of bother at your house, but everything is under control. Inspector Bruce would like to see you when you get back.'

167

Miss Hogg had handed over the telephone to the colonel before the last remark had properly sunk in.

'I wish someone would tell me what this is all about,' she said again.

The colonel said a few more words into the telephone, and then rang off.

'You seem to be a good enough security risk, young lady,' he said. 'The Superintendent vouches for you. Now will you kindly explain how you came to be walking round London with this sample from a uranium mine.'

'And by every indication, a remarkably rich deposit,' added the Professor.

During Miss Hogg's recital of the relevant facts, or such as she thought to be relevant, the three men exchanged glances. Finally the colonel said:

'I think there's no doubt about it, the Russians have found uranium at Chusk, or what used to be called Chusk. With the recent publication of an American Kook that records the fact that Sir Arthur Dewdney visited Chusk in 1870, their Intelligence people have obviously realized that Sir Arthur may have stumbled across something that could reveal the fact to us today.'

'As he did in fact,' said the Professor.

'Strategically, they would have given anything to keep the knowledge from the West,' said the colonel.

'Then you mean,' said Miss Hogg, 'that the Russians may have committed the murder at Miss Emily's?' asked Miss Hogg.

'Or their agents,' said the Colonel.

'We are indebted to this young lady,' said the Professor.

'Is she in any danger?' asked the Director.

'You will have to watch your step for the next few days,' said the colonel. 'And say nothing to anybody about these

– er – stones. I presume you have no objections to handing them over to Professor Burbage?'

'I suppose he's a good security risk?' Miss Hogg asked demurely.

'The best,' the colonel assured her gravely. ' He is in charge of the main Government Research Station at Little Piddling in Dorset.'

CHAPTER 23

At South Green there is only one shop which stands actually on the Green, and that at the extreme south-east corner where the London road, which has cut diagonally across from the north-west, curves round into the former village. It is a pleasant-looking shop, reminiscent of Tunbridge Wells or the Lanes at Brighton, with a discreet Regency front. At one end is a Post Office, there is a grocery counter in the middle, and at the opposite end, stationery and tobacco. Coming back from the Science Museum, Miss Hogg paused to look in at the window, a thing she often did, for Mr. Pauncefoot, the proprietor, had a genius for window display, and each week was responsible for some new creation. On this particular Friday, the *pièce de résistance* in the centre window was a packet of some new brand of detergent, blue ribbons leading from it upwards, and white ribbons downwards, while a hand-lettered placard proclaimed in red letters:

NO BOIL

NO TOIL

Swish

THE NEW WHITER WASHING POWDER

. . .

The left-hand window, as befitted a Government department, bore only a poster urging Miss Hogg to put her money into Savings Certificates, with an inspiring message from Lord Mackintosh which she did not bother to read. In the right-hand window was a display of cigarettes. In the centre of this display was a sort of pagoda made from packets of Player's, while grouped around it were smaller erections built up from Gold Flake packets. And along the bottom of the window ran a row of stubby white packets each bearing a khaki-coloured emblem, which Miss Hogg gazed at with sudden interest. She took off her pince-nez, then jabbed them back on to her nose, and darted into the shop. An old-fashioned bell went 'Ping!' as she passed through the door.

Mr. Pauncefoot was an old friend. He was also a chess addict, and had played many a game with the Superintendent, and now he came forward with a welcoming expression, rubbing his hands and smiling.

'This is a pleasure, Miss Flora.' He was one of the few people who used her Christian name but, like Superintendent Frazer, he had got it from her father who had always used it. 'What can I do for you today?'

'Mr. Pauncefoot, how long have you been selling Camels?'

'Camels, Miss Flora. Oh, for some years now. I didn't know you smoked.'

'I don't. At least, not very much. But Camels are American, aren't they?'

'Definitely. They are one of the best-known American brands, so I have been given to understand.'

Mr. Pauncefoot's tone implied that he hoped it was understood he only stocked the best, whatever the article might be.

'Who buys them in South Green?'

'Well, we got them originally for that American gentleman in Barbrook Lodge. He asked us to stock them three years ago, and his man comes in for a supply every week. But we sell occasional packets to other people, of course. Another American has come to the flats, and he was asking me only the other day for some cigarettes called Luckies. I'm afraid I had to disappoint him.'

'Did he take Camels instead?'

171

'As a matter of fact he did. He took sixty.'

'Bother!' exclaimed Miss Hogg.

Mr. Pauncefoot looked puzzled.

'Just a theory,' said Miss Hogg. She decided to change the subject. 'Have you found anyone else to play chess with?'

'I have a game with your father's successor occasionally, but unfortunately he lives at Twickenham, which is a complication. People don't seem to care much nowadays for the old-fashioned games,' said Mr. Pauncefoot regretfully. 'They want easy amusement, like the wireless and television, which don't require any personal effort.'

'Except the effort to keep awake,' said Miss Hogg. 'Well, thank you very much. I suppose you'd heard I'm a detective now?'

'I had heard a rumour,' Mr. Pauncefoot admitted. 'I'm sure I don't know what your father would have said. But I expect it is more exciting than teaching. That was a very dreadful thing that happened at Miss Emily's,' he added.

'Wasn't it!' Miss Hogg spoke somewhat absently, for she was already evolving a plan. 'Good-bye, Mr. Pauncefoot. If you know anyone who has a crime that wants looking into, you might recommend me.'

' I will, Miss Flora, with the greatest pleasure.' And Mr. Pauncefoot bowed her out of the shop almost as if she had been Miss Emily or even Lady Hounslow.

Miss Hogg was surprised to find a police constable standing by her gate in Acacia Avenue. She became aware also that there was quite a hole in the middle pane of the bay window of the room that was now her office.

'Whatever is going on here?' she asked.

The constable saluted.

'You had a burglar last night,' he said. 'Inspector Bruce has asked me to check over with you if there is anything missing. They broke in at Miss Emily's, too.'

An almost incoherent Milly flew into the hall as she heard Miss Hogg's latchkey in the door.

'Oh, Hogg,' she wailed. 'I must have slept through it all. It's all my fault. I finished off the cherry brandy, and it always makes me sleep like a log. They've made an awful mess of your study, but the inspector said to leave it until you got back.'

Miss Hogg's study was indeed an awful mess. All the drawers in the desk had been taken out, and their contents emptied on the floor. The back of the desk itself had been ripped away with a jemmy or a chisel. The arm-chair had been slashed across the seat and up the back, and most of the stuffing pulled out and scattered over the floor. The carpet had been rolled back, and a loose board at the side of the fireplace had been prised up.

'I can't think why I didn't wake up,' wailed Milly.

'The inspector thinks it's a good job you didn't, miss,' said the constable.

Milly turned quite pale.

'Do – do you think they'd have attacked me?' she asked.

'Not a doubt of it,' said the constable cheerfully. 'The inspector says they're getting desperate.'

'And you say they broke in to Miss Emily's as well?' asked Miss Hogg.

'Yes, miss. The inspector's over there now.'

'We'll go over,' said Miss Hogg to Milly, 'because I have some information for him. Make yourself some tea, officer, while we're away. You'll find all the things in the kitchen.'

'Would you see what's missing first, miss, before you go?'

'Nothing,' said Miss Hogg. 'I can tell you that without looking. Nothing of any importance, that is. I gave what they were looking for to a professor this morning.'

CHAPTER 24

P<small>HYLLIS</small> M<small>AUD</small> let them in at the front door of the Laurels, and it was only too obvious that she was still seething with excitement.

'Oh, miss,' she said, 'we might all have been killed in our beds.' In retrospect, this seemed to afford her the greatest pleasure. 'The murdering villains have smashed up the library. Luckily Miss Emily didn't hear anything this time, because she'd taken two of her tablets.'

'Is she all right?' asked Miss Hogg.

'Cheerful as a cricket,' said Phyllis Maud. 'She's up in the drawing-room with Mr. Bartley Craig, and the inspector's in the library with Sir Wellington Orde.'

'Oh, he's here, is he?'

'The inspector sent a policeman over to fetch him.' Phyllis Maud dropped her voice to a whisper. 'You don't think he could have had anything to do with it, do you, miss?'

'I hardly think so,' replied Miss Hogg. 'The inspector's most probably asking him questions about Sir Arthur, and the things in the library.'

'Did you see my picture in the paper, miss? In the *Star*, it was. You could tell it was me in a minute by my apron. I ought to have took it off by rights.'

'You must show it to me before we go,' said Miss Hogg.

They escaped Phyllis Maud at last, and mounted to the first floor.

'I am so glad you've come,' said Miss Emily, as they entered the drawing-room. 'This is getting rather like a persecution. We shall have to put our heads together. And the inspector tells me they have created almost as much havoc in your house. I am so sorry. I feel quite responsible. Are you insured?'

'I'm insured against burglary,' said Miss Hogg. 'I suppose it counts as a burglary, even if they didn't take anything. But you know how insurance companies always try to get out of it.'

'My dear, it's all really too thrilling,' broke in Mr. Bartley Craig. 'Do you think they've found the treasure, whatever it is?'

'I'm sure they haven't,' said Miss Hogg.

'You sound very confident. I don't see how anyone can know.'

'Forget it,' said Miss Hogg. 'I shouldn't have said it.'

Mr. Bartley Craig gave her a curious look.

'I do believe you know something about it,' he said. 'And you're just being a tease, and hiding it from us.'

'Hogg's going to solve the mystery,' put in Milly loyally.

'I feel quite sure she is,' agreed Miss Emily. 'Have a glass of wine. I'd ask you all to stay to lunch, but I'm afraid Phyllis Maud hardly knows whether she's on her head or her heels.'

'I must be getting back,' said Mr. Bartley Craig. Goodness, it's after one. I haven't finished my article for the *Sunday Mirror.*'

'How's your life of Sir Arthur getting on?' asked Miss Hogg.

Bartley Craig gave her a rather nasty look.

'It's not going at all well,' he said petulantly. 'It hasn't any real news value until you find this ridiculous manuscript. Personally, I don't think there is one.'

There was a tap at the door, followed by the entrance of Phyllis Maud.

'The inspector would like to see Miss Hogg in the library,' she announced importantly.

Bartley Craig accompanied her down the stairs.

'You weren't ever a member of the Communist Party?' asked Miss Hogg suddenly.

'*Dear!*' exclaimed Mr. Bartley Craig. 'I'm sure that's libellous.'

'I haven't put it into writing, I'm only asking you. You've taken up lots of things at one time or another in order to write books about them.'

'Well, I've never been a Communist. Too terribly earnest and uncomfortable, my dear. And everybody going into involuntary liquidation. So *insecure*. Oh, no, it's not my cup of tea at all. But whatever makes you ask?'

'I was thinking about Chusk.'

There was no answering flicker in Mr. Bartley Craig's eyes.

'They call it something else now, but I've forgotten what it is. Like Leningrad, you know. But Communism ceased to be fashionable *years* ago. The thing now is to go over to Rome, like Evelyn and all the rest of them. I've been seriously thinking about it, but I don't think I could bear all that nonsense about confession.'

'I'm sure you couldn't,' said Miss Hogg, and made her way to the library.

The inspector was standing by the window to the right of the fireplace, looking out on to the garden. The library looked as if a hurricane had passed through it. Miss Hogg wondered how Miss Emily could have avoided waking up, and shuddered to think of what might have happened to her if she had.

'I'm sorry about your front room,' said the inspector, turning as she came in. 'But we know what they were looking for now, thanks to you. The Super tells me you've had a session with M.I.5.'

'So that's who Colonel Brassett was. I suppose they told you it was uranium? I didn't really think those stones were anything, or I would have brought them round to you.'

'The theory now is,' said the inspector, 'that all this caper has been to try to prevent us finding the evidence for uranium deposits at Chusk. I don't suppose they knew there was evidence, but they're devilish thorough, and decided to take no chances.'

'If they'd done nothing nobody would ever have found anything until Miss Emily died, and even then the things might have been thrown away.'

'I think there were two lots of people on different jobs,' said the inspector, 'but neither knew what the other was up to. The first lot were probably after the manuscript, and it was they who caused the upset in here before Milligan ever landed.'

'Milligan was after the uranium?'

'It fits in with that text-book of geology we found in his case. And there's a passage in one of Sir Arthur's letters about "the stones to cure rheumatism". That would ring a bell to anyone who was aware of the later developments at Chusk. And the F.B.I., apparently, have been interested in Milligan for some months. I think that's why he disguised himself as a bishop. You don't look too closely into bishops. But I'm as certain as can be he had a confederate in London, and very probably here in South Green.'

Miss Hogg seated herself on the central table, one of the few articles in the library to remain entirely undamaged.

'You don't suspect Sir Wellington Orde, do you?'

'Almost anyone may be a Russian agent. Sometimes it's a matter of ideology, and sometimes it's simply a matter of money. But I've had his story, and I'm inclined to accept it. I think he was after the manuscript.'

He went on to tell her of Lord Hounslow's telephone call, and of his interview with that venerable peer and his friend, Mr. Mountjoy.

'I couldn't see Sir Wellington last night, he'd gone up to town to a dinner, so I asked him to come over and see me here this morning. I told him that Mr. Mountjoy had seen him, and I showed him the pencil we had found, and he agreed it was his. Then I cautioned him, and asked him if he cared to make a statement. He said he had simply been taking a stroll round the Green before going to bed, and he had jumped into the drive here when Mountjoy's headlights flashed on because they momentarily dazzled him, and he thought the car was nearer than it was, and was coming for him. He admitted that he'd been round the house and into the garden, but says he never went close enough to the library window to notice anything, and in any case the curtains were drawn.'

'Could you be sure of that from the garden?'

'I don't know. We should have to try it out at dark. But what makes me incline to believe his story is he says he suddenly smelled tobacco smoke – Turkish or Egyptian, he described it – and he had a feeling there was someone in the garden, and he bolted for home.'

'That was the person who had begun to smoke the Camel?'

'I think so. He couldn't possibly know we had found a Camel in the clump of bushes there.'

'I found a partly smoked Camel in room number five at the Brontë hotel,' remarked Miss Hogg.

'The devil you did!'

Miss Hogg recounted her conversation with Rene.

'Then he did have a visitor,' said the inspector. 'I was sure someone had met him on his arrival in London. The only thing that's bothering me is why Milligan had to come into it at all.'

'Perhaps Milligan was the head of the organization,' suggested Miss Hogg.

'Oh, he was. But you'd think he could leave the dirty work to his lieutenants.'

'He may not have trusted them.'

'Could be. We have two lines to go on. One that he was murdered by his own gang for some reason, and the other that someone after the manuscript fell foul of him and did him in. Against that is the fact that we'd decided he must have known whoever it was who hit him.'

'Well, I must take Milly home to lunch,' said Miss Hogg, 'and then try and clear up the front room. I shall have to get the window put in, too.'

'I shall have a constable at your place tonight, and one here,' said the inspector. 'These American gangsters stick at nothing.'

CHAPTER 25

Miss Hogg was sunk in abstraction during the rather late lunch which Milly threw together on their return to Acacia Avenue. She toyed absently with the runny scrambled egg, the more runny because Milly had incorporated in the mixture two watery tomatoes (from the Canary Islands) 'in order to save their lives', as she had explained, and first refused and then took some of the jam Milly passed over on discovering that she had not yet eaten the slice of bread she had buttered to go with the egg.

'I've come to the conclusion,' she said, as she stirred her coffee which brought the collation to an end, 'that the murderer was an accomplice. Milligan scouted round in the daytime, as the bishop, and I expect he had hoped to do a bit of searching, only there were too many people in and out all the time. But he must have arranged to meet the accomplice while at the Brontë hotel. He never openly communicated with anyone after that.'

'And who was it?' asked Milly, who had been listening breathless to all this.

'The only person left it could be is Shumacher,' said Miss Hogg decisively. 'And I've got a plan.'

'Oh, Hogg, do be careful. You know what the inspector said.'

'If I'm not back by five o'clock you can ring the inspector and tell him I've gone to call on Shumacher and not returned,' said Miss Hogg. 'I have to go to Richmond first. Where's that little attaché-case I used to have for picnics?'

It was a quarter past three when she set out for Richmond, carrying a small square attaché-case made of reinforced cardboard. Arrived at Richmond, she began a round of tobacconists. At the first two she was unlucky, and the assistants looked after her as she marched out after making her abortive requests with some shaking of the head and shrugging of the shoulders. But at the third she was able to secure what she wanted.

'Have you any unpopular brand of American cigarettes?' she asked the assistant at the third shop, a gawky young man whose most noticeable feature was a prominent Adam's apple. 'I want something really cheap and nasty.'

'I don't know about cheap, miss. We have a line that doesn't sell very well.' He turned to a cupboard with a glass door just behind him, and from one of the shelves produced a squat white packet decorated with the Stars and Stripes.

'These are called Old Glory, miss,' he said, 'and we don't sell many of them. In fact,' he added, in a burst of candour, 'we haven't sold any of them at all. Would they be what you are wanting?'

'The very thing,' said Miss Hogg. 'I want ten packets.'

'Certainly, miss. Shall I wrap them up for you?'

'No, they can go in my case.' She opened it as she spoke, revealing nothing but a reporter's note-book and a ball-pointed pen.

Even the fact that she only received a few shillings back in return for three pound notes did not appear to damp her spirits. She bade the assistant an affable good afternoon, and made for the Quadrant, to take a bus back to South Green.

The bus put her down only twenty yards from Mr. Pauncefoot's shop. With hardly a glance at its windows, she walked round on to the Green and along South Side until she reached the corner where the telephone box was. The church clock showed the time to be twenty minutes to five. She proceeded up East Side, passing Sir Wellington Orde's gate, and then Lady Martyngale's, and finally arrived at Barbrook Lodge. The front of the house was separated from the roadway by a high brick wall above which was a

181

tangle of yew. At one time the yews had been cut square but, neglected for some years, they had branched out into jagged and uneven shapes. The gate in the wall, which was of solid board coated with flaking brown paint, opened with difficulty, and admitted her to a grass grown stretch of gravel. The house itself was equally unprepossessing. It was a squat, two-storied erection of the late Victorian period, and the grey stucco had weathered badly, while the door and windows looked as if they had received their last coat of paint in some remote period before the war.

Miss Hogg marched resolutely up the short drive, climbed the three grimy and lichen-covered steps, and rang the front door bell. It was of the old-fashioned kind, a rusty iron knob connected by wire with a bell which she could hear jangling in the depths of the house. It stopped, and silence descended again. She heard a car in the distance, and then that, too, faded away. Miss Hogg shivered involuntarily. 'Someone walking over my grave,' she said, and gave a second pull at the bell. And almost instantly the door was thrown open.

The man who confronted her was not a very attractive specimen of humanity, though a certain amount of personal effort could have improved him a little. His most noticeable feature was a broken nose, set in the middle of a face the colour of tallow. It was obvious that he had not shaved for a day or two and Miss Hogg, who was trained to notice the ebb and flow of the tide of hygiene on a pupil's neck and behind her ears, was more than doubtful whether he had had a wash during the same period. His simian eyes took in Miss Hogg, and then he spoke.

'What yous want?'

'Is Mr. Shumacher in?'

'He don't see no punk callers.'

'Oh, I'm sure he'll see me.'

Her confidence seemed to shake the man. He had been on the point of closing the door in her face, but Miss Hogg had got her case open, and he waited for one fatal instant to discover what she was about to produce.

With a clumsy movement, Miss Hogg caused the case to tip over sideways, and half a dozen packets of Old Glory cigarettes were ejected over the other's feet. One packet shot past him into the hall.

'I'm travelling in a new brand of cigarette,' explained Miss Hogg glibly. The man with the broken nose had lowered his guard for a split second, and Miss Hogg was already through the door, and retrieving the packet she had lost. 'Most Americans smoke Camels or Luckies,' she went on. 'Now Old Glory have everything that they have got, and far more besides. They are sterilized and – er – deodorized, and the tobacco has all been predigested by a new patent process so that it is absolutely harmless while preserving the fullest aroma.'

'What is all this?' asked a new voice from immediately behind her.

Miss Hogg, who had paused for breath, turned to find a tall, thin man standing in the doorway of the room to the right of the front door. His hair was cut *en brosse* in the German fashion, and he was wearing dark glasses which were somehow rather alarming.

'Our firm,' said Miss Hogg, 'wants you to try a sample packet of these cigarettes, and then to let us have your candid opinion of them.'

'This is foolishness,' said the man in the doorway. 'Come in here.'

Snapping shut the lid of her attaché-case, her heart thumping faster than usual though outwardly self-possessed, Miss Hogg followed the man into the room from which he had emerged. It looked to Miss Hogg more like a bar parlour than a living-room. In the centre of the floor was a table with a green baize top on which were two packs of cards, one stacked, and the other thrown down with the cards scattered, as if someone had been interrupted when about to deal. On the table were two glasses, and an array of bottles stood on a small sideboard in the background. By the fire were two leather arm-chairs, and her host indicated one of them.

'Sit please.'

As she took the nearest chair she glanced over her shoulder. The man with the broken nose had come into the room, and was standing in front of the closed door.

'I am advertising Old Glory cigarettes,' began Miss Hogg, with rather less assurance, but she was interrupted.

'Let us cease this foolishness, please. You come to spy.'

'To spy what?' asked Miss Hogg, with well-simulated astonishment.

'What your game is I don't know.' The man with the dark glasses spoke with a strong American accent, though occasionally his constructions betrayed some foreign language as his native tongue. Probably German, thought Miss Hogg. 'Perhaps it is that you just like to meddle. To poke in the nose for what you call fun. But I am sorry to say you may find it is not such fun.'

'Am I right in thinking you are Mr. Shumacher?'

'That is my name.'

'Then you're German?'

'I am an American citizen, though, if it interests you, I was born in Switzerland.'

'Then I suppose you've adopted your mother's name,' said Miss Hogg reflectively, 'and your father's name was really Bonelli?'

The face of the man who called himself Shumacher had gone quite blank. His mouth set in a thin line. His eyes were invisible behind the dark glasses.

'I think you are a very foolish person,' he said.

It suddenly struck Miss Hogg that if she were indeed in the presence of Milligan's murderer, she was in a position of considerable danger. She glanced at the clock in the centre of the mantelpiece. In ten minutes, Milly would be ringing the inspector. She must keep things going for twenty minutes or so. For one moment she wondered what would happen if the inspector chanced to be out, but surely Milly, on the warpath, would not give up until she had got through to the Superintendent, and he would hesitate no more than would the inspector. She had not wanted to frighten Milly, and the only thing she hoped was that she had impressed five o'clock sufficiently vividly on the other's mind.

'I suppose you were after the black pebbles that Sir Arthur found,' she said conversationally. Shumacher could not possibly know yet that they had been handed over to Professor Burbage.

'What do you know about them?' Shumacher was instantly all attention.

'I forget where Sir Arthur was supposed to have found them, but he said the natives regarded them as a cure for rheumatism.'

Her host, who had been standing all this time, now took the chair opposite her.

'You interest me profoundly,' he said. 'Where are these stones?'

'I might make an exchange,' said Miss Hogg. 'There are one or two things that have puzzled me.'

'Such as?' Shumacher's intonation was sarcastic.

'Why did you tear those pages from the back of Sir Arthur's note-book?'

'They were blank pages, of no importance, but my colleague made on them some beautiful impressions of his fingers, due to the grime which Miss Dewdney's servant seems to permit everywhere –'

'That's hardly fair,' Miss Hogg interrupted him, leaping to the defence of Phyllis Maud. 'The boxes hadn't been touched for ages. And besides, Miss Emily dusts the library herself.'

'I thought it best to remove the few pages on which his prints were so clearly outlined. There was nothing in the note-book itself of any interest.'

'Nothing about a manuscript?'

'I care nothing about a manuscript. We are not interested in it.'

Only by the exercise of iron control could Miss Hogg stop herself glancing again at the clock. Milly must even now be telephoning the police station.

'But the main thing is,' she said, 'why did you kill Milligan?'

The man opposite looked genuinely astonished.

'But I did not kill Milligan. Why should I? He was killed by a former partner who was looking for your ridiculous manuscript.'

'Who was that?' asked Miss Hogg. The whole thing seemed to be getting beyond her again.

'Why, Hamsen, whom we used to call Dough Face – the man you know as Professor Amos T. Hoade.'

CHAPTER 26

Miss Hogg sat quite still for a moment, turning everything over in her mind. At the same time another part of her brain was repeating over and over again the phrase 'Five minutes to go'. The clock ticked away on the mantelpiece.

'I'd always imagined,' she said, with a glance over her shoulder at the man with the broken nose who was still standing silently with his back to the door, 'that your friend here was Dough Face.'

'My friend here was not at Harvard like Hamsen,' said Shumacher. 'It would not be easy for him to imitate the college professor.'

'I suppose not,' said Miss Hogg absently. She took off her pince-nez, and rubbed them vigorously with her handkerchief.

'You were going to tell me where are the black pebbles,' said her companion, leaning forward. His tone was distinctly menacing.

' Of course,' said Miss Hogg. 'But do tell me first, why did you let Hamsen kill Milligan?'

'How did I know he would do so foolish a thing?' asked the other angrily. 'I watch in the garden while Milligan searches, and suddenly I see Hamsen at the window. I think they have perhaps, arranged a rendezvous, and they do not tell me. I wait a moment, and then I hear a cry. I run to the window, and as I climb in, Hamsen goes through the door and escapes. I see Milligan is already dead. The house is awake, and I hear Miss Dewdney calling out. There is nothing I can do. I go home.'

It was at this moment that the bell in the hall jangled into life, and a thunderous knocking could be heard on the outer door. Almost on the instant, Shumacher had drawn a gun and was pointing it at Miss Hogg.

'I think that's rather rude,' she said, trying to appear unconcerned.

'Silence!' hissed the other.

The man with the broken nose had gone from the room, closing the door behind him. The front door could be heard opening, and she distinguished a voice which she knew to be the inspector's.

'It would be silly to start firing guns,' she observed to Shumacher. 'There's no future in it.' Very deliberately she got to her feet and smoothed down her tweed skirt. 'That's the police, you know. If Hoade or Hamsen as you call him did the murder, I can't see why you're worried. They can only deport you for being a Russian spy.'

Shumacher had also got to his feet, but he had replaced the gun under his arm. The inspector's voice could be heard quite clearly from the hall.

'I'm in here, Inspector,' cried Miss Hogg, and immediately the door was flung open to reveal the inspector followed by a uniformed sergeant.

'Thank God, you're all right,' said the inspector.

'Be careful, he's got a gun,' said Miss Hogg. 'And he did the murder all right.'

Shumacher made a quick movement, but the sergeant was quicker. He had the man's arms in a lock behind his back, and the gun flew across the room.

'He's told me a wonderful fairy story,' explained Miss Hogg to the inspector. 'But I realized it was all wrong. You remember I said the library had been just like a railway station? Well, he missed out Sir Wellington Orde. If you ask me, it was a simple case of when thieves fall out. Shumacher here, whose real name is Bonelli, must have resented the fact of Milligan's taking control again. And I think there'd been trouble about dividing the loot on a previous occasion, which was why they split up.'

'I'd got a warrant for his arrest on a charge of breaking and entering,' said the inspector. 'He did all the damage last night. The F.B.I. let us know only an hour ago that his real name is Bonelli, and he's known to have been in contact with the Russians.'

'I shouldn't be at all surprised if he wasn't after the manuscript as well. Two birds with one stone, you know. You see this book of Professor Hoade's cousin had in it a letter mentioning the rheumatism cure – and I expect the Chusk peasantry, if there are any left, still use the same word for it – but it had far more in it about the manuscript. Which reminds me, I must fly. Dr. Greenwood will have arrived. I'll let you know if we find the manuscript.'

'I shall have to call round and see you later,' said the inspector.

'Oh, by the way,' said Miss Hogg, coming back into the room and tipping out the contents of her case on to the table. 'Could you dispose of these?' She lifted up one of the packets of Old Glory. 'They look very nice, but the man I got them from didn't recommend them very highly. Perhaps they'd do for the Police Orphanage, or something like that.'

Her quickest way home lay along North Side, and as she reached the far corner, she decided to dash into the Laurels, and let Miss Emily know that the case was over.

Miss Emily was extremely gratified to hear the news. The last few days, culminating in the sack of the library, had been a considerable strain, even though she had shown few outward signs of it.

'I think I'll put some of the manuscripts into my case, and take them round for Dr. Greenwood to look at in my house,' said Miss Hogg, suddenly realizing that Miss Emily was in no condition to suffer a further invasion that evening. 'I'll be very careful of them and, of course, Dr. Greenwood is an expert.'

189

'Take anything you like, my dear. I am more than grateful for all you have done.' Miss Emily held out her hand. 'I won't come down, but we must have a business talk in the morning.'

Dr. Greenwood was coming up Acacia Avenue from the farther end as Miss Hogg turned in at the other from Barbrook Drive. They met at her gate. Owing to the state of the front room, Miss Hogg had to take him into the living-room, at the back where she introduced him to Milly. Dr. Greenwood, in a tone which would not have carried conviction to an attentive listener, said that he remembered her perfectly.

'We've just arrested the murderer,' said Miss Hogg, throwing her rather shapeless hat on to the windowsill. 'I always knew it was Shumacher,' she added complacently. 'Simply because it couldn't have been anybody else. He tried to tell me it was Professor Hoade, but he obviously didn't know a thing about Sir Wellington Orde.'

Dr. Greenwood looked puzzled.

'Sir Wellington Orde was surely not involved?'

'He was taking a walk in Miss Emily's garden at the critical moment,' explained Miss Hogg. 'And I wouldn't put it past him to have had a penknife, and even be meditating a private browse in Miss Emily's library.' Dr. Greenwood looked shocked. 'Shumacher had waited until Milligan got engrossed in the boxes – he was supposed to be keeping *cave* – and then he followed him in and murdered him. I think he'd started on a cigarette while he was waiting, and he threw it down, and it was the smell of it frightened Sir Wellington away. Unless it turns out he actually saw something, but I don't suppose he'll ever open up about that.'

'But surely,' said Milly, who had been following all this with the closest interest, 'Shumacher must have known he couldn't pin it on to Professor Hoade.'

'He thought I would believe it, and make the inspector believe it, just long enough for him to make his getaway. He probably has a private aeroplane at some club near London. It's only a few hours to the nearest stretch of the Iron Curtain. I should have believed him, of course, if he hadn't missed out Sir Wellington. And then it was obvious he must be the murderer.'

'You are wonderful, Hogg,' said Milly.

'They would have been well away by the time the inspector had finished questioning Professor Hoade, and checking up on him with the F.B.I. Especially as Professor Hoade has a guilt complex about the manuscript. I'm sure, really, he was hoping to find it, and I doubt he'd have told Miss Emily.'

'Ah, yes, the manuscript,' put in Dr. Greenwood, who had been listening to these exchanges with some impatience, and appeared plainly bored with the murder.

'I've brought a selection,' said Miss Hogg, opening her case. 'I thought we wouldn't bother Miss Emily tonight, but these will give you an idea of the sort of things they are. Put the light on, Milly. It's so dark at the back here.'

Milly switched on the reading-lamp, which was on top of the sewing-machine behind Dr. Greenwood's chair, and its melancholy brown glow fell on Dr. Greenwood's bald head.

'We forgot to change the shade back,' said Milly.

Dr. Greenwood had screwed himself round in his chair, and was gazing up at the lampshade in astonishment. He took a glass out of his pocket, and got up without speaking.

'What ghastly vandalism is this?' he asked. He bent over the shade. 'Great heavens! This appears to be a palimpsest of the early second century.'

Miss Hogg looked at Milly, and Milly looked at Miss Hogg.

'Do – do you mean it might be valuable?'

'Valuable!' snorted Dr. Greenwood. 'In monetary terms I could make no estimate. But in another sense, it may be priceless. It will have to be photographed. The later writing is from the *Consolations*, I think.' He gave a little moan. 'We must separate the pages very, very carefully.'

CHAPTER 27

It was Monday when Dr. Greenwood rang up Miss Hogg. His voice was quivering with emotion.

'Do you know what this manuscript is?' he asked.

'I haven't a clue,' said Miss Hogg, a somewhat regrettable expression she had picked up from the girls of the County High School.

Dr. Greenwood's voice took on a note of reverence. He might have been a B.B.C. announcer communicating the news of the sudden death of a top-flight performer in the world of sport.

'It is the lost ending of St. Mark's Gospel,' he said.

'I never knew it had lost its ending,' remarked Miss Hogg. 'You mean it's quite a find?'

Dr. Greenwood made a number of spluttering noises, and at last became intelligible again.

'It's absolutely priceless,' he said. 'Priceless. It's not only the earliest manuscript of the Gospels in existence, but it's one that has been lost for nearly nineteen centuries.'

Miss Hogg was silent for a moment.

'We were talking about it only this morning at Miss Emily's,' she said. 'She says she has no wish to make any money out of it, but if it's worth presenting anywhere, she would like to present it, on condition it bears some sort of ticket giving Sir Arthur's name.'

'Worth presenting –' Words again failed Dr. Greenwood.

'I suggested you might like it for the Burghley Library,' went on Miss Hogg. 'It would sort of balance the Harland Bequest.'